THE MENACE

MICKEY SPILLANE
MAX ALLAN COLLINS

ROUGH
EDGES
PRESS

Rough Edges Press
An Imprint of Wolfpack Publishing
5130 S. Fort Apache Rd. 215-380
Las Vegas, NV 89148

roughedgespress.com

Paperback ISBN 978-1-68549-072-0
LCCN 2022933131

In memory of
JOE KANE
Phantom of the Movies

"Stephen King. Now I'm not crazy about him, but he's a great writer."

Mickey Spillane

THE MENACE

A BRIEF INTRODUCTION TO THE MENACE

BY THE CO-AUTHOR

In 2006, following her late husband's instructions, Jane Spillane turned over the files of Mickey Spillane's unfinished, unpublished materials to me. He had told her, "Max will know what to do."

In the subsequent decade and a half I have completed twelve Mike Hammer novels, working from material ranging from a manuscript lacking only a few chapters to one-page synopses, as well as two non-Hammer novels and a number of short stories both with and without his famous private eye. I concentrated on Hammer as, obviously, Mike was Mickey's signature character. Not coincidentally, this book is being published during the 75th anniversary of Mike Hammer's first appearance in the novel *I, the Jury* (1947).

Toward that end I am including, as a back-of-the-book bonus feature of sorts, the newly discovered original version of the only full-length Mike Hammer short story Mickey ever wrote. More about that, later....

Most of the material in Mickey's files ran to substantial portions of novels he'd begun and set aside for a variety of reasons. The files contained fragments ranging from a few chapters to a few pages and even a few paragraphs. Among the few completed works were three unproduced non-Hammer screenplays. One, a western he'd written for his friend John Wayne, I novelized as *The Legend of Caleb York* and followed with (to date) five more Caleb York novels. Two more screenplays remained, and this book represents one of them.

I am not sure what Mickey intended for *The Menace*, as its length was rather short, indicating possibly a pilot for an anthology TV series of horror yarns designed for a one-hour time slot with commercials. I do know he was excited about it and hoped to produce it himself. He'd written it shortly before he and I became friends after we appeared together at a Bouchercon (the traveling convention for mystery fans and professionals) in Milwaukee in 1981.

The quote about Stephen King that I've included as an epigram is typically pithy of Mickey, but it requires explanation. Mickey, the bestselling American mystery writer of the Twentieth Century, was keenly aware of other singular writers whose popularity reached the same stratosphere as his own. In the final decades of his life, Mickey was almost semi-retired, only publishing occasionally, but someone with King's astonishing popularity caught his attention...and the Mick was frequently asked his opinion about the newcomer.

Mickey had enormous respect for Stephen King's storytelling ability as well as popularity, achieved in part by shrewd marketing, which included building a popular persona that had made the young writer a multi-media star...much as had been the case for Mickey, who stayed a celebrity long after he'd stopped publishing regularly.

When Mickey said he was "not crazy" about King, but that King was "a great writer," Mike Hammer's creator was being typically cryptic. When I pressed him about it, he explained he was referring to the supernatural subject matter that the author of *Carrie* often explored.

Mickey Spillane, as sometimes surprises people, was a very religious man, and conservatively so. He stopped writing his trademark sex-and-violence Hammer yarns for a decade after converting to the Jehovah's Witnesses, and returned only during a period when he and his church were on the outs. Later, when he was back in the fold, Mickey struggled to write novels (including two Hammers) that would not put him at odds with his church or, for that matter, his fans. And he was uncomfortable with any demonic subjects in fiction (*The Exorcist* for example).

Actually he believed in such things and did not consider the occult anything to be fooled around with.

But Mickey was acutely aware of the rising popularity of horror fiction in the '70s and early '80s—thanks to Stephen King—and *The Menace* was his response. His horror yarn, as one might expect, was conceived in mystery / crime-novel terms, and with a founding in the real, not the supernatural.

Mickey was a circus buff who at times performed with both Clyde Beatty and Ringling Brothers, getting shot out of a cannon and doing trampoline stunts. Among the circus folk he knew and valued were sideshow performers—some called, in the parlance of the day, "freaks." He knew of one such individual, born with deformities, who could convincingly portray the title "monster." His script included references to attached photos of his friend, which unfortunately were no longer attached when it came into my hands.

He spoke to me numerous times of his excitement for this project, though—as I say—I'm not sure exactly what format he had in mind. He intended not only to produce, but possibly to direct it himself.

For now, I've created a version in the medium that made Mickey the Stephen King of his generation: the novel. I have not greatly expanded it, though I have attempted to expand it in ways I believe he would have, had the project gone into production (or even, for that matter, pre-production). The rather short script may have been intended to be a quick read for fund-raising purposes, and rather than augment it with new story elements, I have tried to honor Mickey's intentions here, while creating a more fleshed-out setting and back stories for the characters.

For the purposes of this narrative, the action takes place when Mickey wrote it—the late 1970s. A mildly mentally challenged character in the novel is discussed in terms and attitudes consistent with those times.

Max Allan Collins
Muscatine, Iowa
June 2021

CHAPTER 1

The day the doctor died began well.

Retired obstetrician Vernon Petersen, 75, awoke at six as usual, almost eerily on the dot despite his never setting an alarm. After a yawn and a stretch, he swung out of bed and began his morning ritual with the usual regimen of pills, orange juice, oatmeal, one cup of black coffee and a slice of the *Today* show with Tom Brokaw. Once feeling fully ready to take on the world—or at least his three friends in their regular foursome at the Peachtree Heights Country Club—he took care of his toiletries (he preferred bathing to showering) and got dressed.

Vernon no longer felt the malaise that had for six long months been his uninvited companion since the death of his beloved wife, Jean. Their condo with its scenic view of the Chattahoochee River suddenly had seemed unnecessarily large without her in it. The cancer had come for her quick, which was merciful in a way, but after fifty years of marriage made for a long recovery for the spouse left behind.

His three kids were grown and gone, none of them in

the South any longer and he sensed their invitations to come live with their respective families—and both his boy and each of the two girls had offered—would only be a prelude to a nursing home. No one wanted a seventy-five year-old man to move in with them. At their stage of life, *he* wouldn't have either.

His only concession to his grief was to place Jean's framed picture—each a different one, at various stages of her life, lovely at any age—in every room of this very modern condo filled with her antique furnishings. And he still talked to her, out loud, a habit he did not consider worth breaking. Having her picture to smile at him as he groused about this and that was a comfort.

Dr. Vernon Petersen was a man of average height with a full head of white hair and decent eyesight, even now requiring only reading glasses. In his day, he'd heard it said he resembled Robert Taylor, but knew that wasn't true anymore. And, anyway, no one remembered who Robert Taylor was these days, outside of Vernon's own age group. He took no exercise other than golf, though if it got too cold for that in the winter months, he substituted regular walks. That was all, but his stomach was flat and he hadn't been a smoker for thirty years and never a heavy drinker. A glass of wine before bed. Maybe a cocktail dining out.

In a pink short-sleeve polo and cream-color shorts, he set out for the country club. Soon he and the other three retired doctors were playing their regular eighteen holes in the crisp October air. The four men were evenly matched and all regularly scored in the low 90s. This made the competition friendly yet fierce.

Today Vernon shot 88 and felt like Arnold Palmer. The other three gave him crap, but they were clearly pleased for him. Only Merle seemed somewhat annoyed, but then he was one of those golfers who scored only misery on the course yet kept coming back for more.

Which of course Vernon and the others found endlessly amusing.

The four finished up around noon and took their regular lunch at their regular table in the clubhouse dining room. Their standing order was steak sandwiches and fries all around, after cocktails of course (Vernon usually just had a Coke, today no exception). Like many doctors, they didn't eat particularly healthy, and Vernon was the only non-smoker. But at least his fellow physicians didn't puff away at the table until after the meal.

All four men wore pastel polos and cream-color shorts and golf caps that they were classy enough to remove in the dining room, making them an exception.

"You know," Walter Johnson said, a heavy-set retired heart surgeon who'd performed Vernon's double bypass, "we're getting to be a dying breed around this neck of the woods."

"Who is?" Vernon asked.

Walter raised an untamed eyebrow. "You heard about Sam Carter."

"No." Vernon shrugged. "Haven't kept in touch since he retired. He's in Atlanta, isn't he?"

Short stumpy Merle, an ophthalmologist, grunted, adjusting his glasses on the bridge of his bump of a nose. "He's in the *ground* is where he is. You didn't hear? Don't you take the paper?"

"I take the paper, but I didn't hear."

"Fell down his goddamn stairs," Jack Matheson said. The retired oncologist was Vernon's height, bald, a one-time high school quarterback whose chin had long since disappeared into his neck, though only a protruding gut had otherwise impacted his physique.

"You're lucky," Merle said to Vernon, "that you only have one floor in that place of yours."

"Well, Sam Carter, huh," Vernon said, summoning a frown. "Isn't that a damn shame."

Actually, Carter—a recently retired pediatric surgeon who used devices to straighten limbs, a procedure that struck Vernon as sadistic—had been an awful man.

"Oh, he was a prick," Merle said dismissively. "What's a *shame* is what happened to Lee Meyer."

Vernon nodded.

That death he knew about—it had made the local TV news and the paper. Meyer, also retired though not recently, had been a pediatrician. He'd gone out fishing on his cabin cruiser by himself (never a good idea) and had apparently fallen overboard and drowned. His boat had been found turning in a circle and he was washed up on shore. This was last week, and Vernon had almost gone to the funeral.

Walter, who had a dry, dark sense of humor, said, "Maybe we're okay. Maybe it's only retired *kid* doctors God has it in for."

"Two accidental deaths," Vernon said, a little disturbed by this talk, "isn't an epidemic."

"No, but still—it makes you think."

"Does it?" Merle smirked. "About what? Not walkin' down the stairs? Not goin' out on the river? You gotta live your friggin' life!"

"Till it's over you do," Walter said with a slight smile. "Then you can take the day off."

Jack grinned. "Retired people take *every* day off."

"Bullshit!" Merle said. "I've never been busier! My wife works me like a damn dog, like a goddamn dog! And I spend half my time babysitting the grandkids."

Vernon smiled. "And you love it."

Merle shrugged. "Yeah. I do. My point is, you can't go through life like it's a damn mine field."

"But you should," Walter said. The heart surgeon was big on diet and exercise, though he was lighting up his latest cigarette as he made this remark.

"What you *should* do," Jack said, "is live every day like it's your last." The oncologist had been the one who discovered Jean's cancer.

Walter started coughing, the smoke going down the wrong way. "You mean like I do?" he said, still coughing, and everybody laughed at that.

Back at the condo, Vernon took a nap. Then, returning to the world about an hour later, he watched *The Match Game* before starting the latest Sidney Sheldon novel, which he read until it was time to get decked out for his big night.

That big night was his third date with Jessica Hahn, the widow of his car dealership buddy Norm—actually, Vernon's third date period, since Jean's death. Right now he felt much as he had anticipating the previous two dates—exhilarated...and guilty.

In the hospital, in what would soon be her death bed, his lovely bride of fifty years had looked at him with those eyes as clear and blue as ever they'd been and said, "You need to date."

"What?" he'd blurted.

"When I'm gone, you're not to be lonely. I won't have it. Promise me."

"You're not going anywhere."

"Of course I am. And so are you, just a little later than me. I want you to promise me you won't be lonely and just sit around and mope."

That was from a song in *Damn Yankees*, a musical they both loved. She'd played the lead in college—Lola, who got whatever she wanted—and had been wonderful in the sexy role. He hadn't known her, just another guy in the audience. But he'd gone out of his way to remedy that.

"Sure, baby," he told her.

She squeezed his hand, harder than a woman dying of cancer should be able to. "*Promise* me."

"Sure. Sure."

But for almost six months, he hadn't kept that promise. He in fact did, as she'd predicted, sit around and mope; also weep his eyes and heart and guts out. He'd gone around the place talking to her picture in every room and went to the cemetery every whip stitch and put on LPs of their favorite songs and watched old movies on TV that they'd seen first-run together. He would talk to his kids on the phone and pretend to be fine. And then he would cry and feel sorry for himself.

One small solace were the people who came up to him not to offer condolences—usually not even knowing about Jean's passing—but folks twenty through fifty, with thanks and smiles at running into the doctor who'd brought their children or sometimes themselves into the world. It was the kind of thing that made a life of doctoring seem not only worthwhile, but special.

That wasn't enough to warm a night, but it was something. Momentary, but something.

He ran into Jessica at the supermarket. She'd lost Norm a year ago. Ten years younger than Vernon, she looked very nice, her hair a believable blonde, her figure full but in a really good way. She did nice things to her yellow and black patterned polyester top and yellow flared slacks. She might have been forty, not sixty-something.

They chatted in the frozen food aisle. Pointedly, they said nothing about their respective late spouses. They asked each other what they'd been doing with themselves, and he was playing a lot of golf and she was in three bridge clubs.

But then she said, "Do you know what I miss?"

"No."

"Going out to eat. Seeing shows. Movies. Plays. Just...getting out."

So they'd been to the movies twice—*The Spy Who Loved Me* and *Sinbad and the Eye of the Tiger*. They shared popcorn. He kissed her after the second date, and realized he'd sort of forgotten how.

That evening they went to *Oh, God!* Which, coincidentally, is what she said, seeing he'd worn a denim leisure suit that accidentally matched her pant suit.

After, she invited him in for wine and they sat on her couch in a condo not unlike his, only no antique furniture. They kissed and petted a little, like the teenagers they'd been long ago, though not together at the time. Yet they were of similar enough ages to have shared the past. Finally she took him into her bedroom, where a photo had been turned face down, and she undressed. She gave him a low-lighting look at her at sixty-five and he undressed.

It hadn't taken more than maybe ten minutes, from soup to nuts, and was wholly unremarkable as sexual experiences go, but he hadn't felt this happy for a long time. When he started to cry, she just held him and patted him like the child he'd been even longer ago.

"You can stay the night," she told him, when he finally swung around to sit on the edge of the bed.

"Not quite ready for that," he said.

"Okay." Her smile was small but he sensed she was relieved, not hurt. They'd gone from sharing popcorn to sharing her bed awfully fast, after all. They might have to back up now before moving forward.

In a robe, she walked him across her living room to

her door as if they were outside and he was walking her to hers.

"That was wonderful," he told her.

"It was." She was smiling that same not-quite-sad smile.

They hugged.

With some spring in his step, guilt and elation wrestling to a draw, he strode to his car, a 1975 Ford Granada he'd bought from her late husband. They waved to each other and then he was driving away, feeling as if he'd been struck by a pleasant piano falling from a window.

In the condo, he took a shower this time and thought about how so many days just slid by blurring into the next, but this one, wow, this was a keeper. If God let him live one day over, out of these last six months, this would be it.

He got into some black silk pajamas Jean had bought him and didn't even feel sheepish doing so. In his bare feet, he padded out to the kitchen, got himself a glass of Chardonnay and settled into his recliner to watch Johnny Carson. He didn't always make it through Johnny, and if it was a guest host never, and often would wind up halfway through the night sleeping in the La-Z-Boy.

Not this time. He even watched some of the late news. And when he crawled into the queen-size bed, feeling only a twinge of guilt from his wife's absence under these familiar sheets and covers, he had to read more Sidney Sheldon for half an hour before the euphoria of being with a woman again had worn off enough for him to set his reading glasses on the bedside stand, hit the light and drift off.

Then something woke him.

It felt immediate, but it wasn't. The clock said 3:35, so he'd been asleep well over an hour, almost two. But a noise had interrupted a dream already forgotten, both the specific dream and specific noise, gone—leaving just the sensation of being jerked from somewhere else.

He leaned on an elbow and listened.

Nothing.

But he remained in a sitting position. He was not a light sleeper. It really took something to wake him. Of course, it might have been outside, an animal disturbing a garbage can, a car backfiring, drunken kids partying, any damn thing, if it was loud enough.

Only now...nothing.

He patted his pillow and drew the sheet and blankets up around him. Turning on his side, he willed thoughts away, other than a general sense that he wouldn't mind returning to the pleasant dream whose specifics he'd lost....

This time he was not quite asleep when a noise sat him up straight in bed.

It sounded like a chair had been bumped in the kitchen!

What was it—had a damn raccoon gotten into the place or some damn thing? Or perhaps some unwanted company on *two* legs....

He threw the blankets off, and stared into the darkness for a few moments, enough moonlight from the windows on the river to give him more or less immediate night vision. Yet that wasn't enough, so he clicked on the bedside lamp and swung around to sit on the edge of the bed. Frowning, he thrust his feet into his slippers.

For a long time he'd kept a gun, a Colt .38 revolver, in his bedside drawer. But he'd moved it to the bottom of the dresser, under a bunch of clothes, after he'd almost used the gun on himself a few weeks after Jean's passing. He believed in having a gun in the house, of being able to defend oneself in one's home. And drug addicts from time to time broke into doctors' homes looking for supplies—that was common, though it had never happened to him.

So he'd shifted the .38 to the bottom dresser drawer to give himself fairly close access but at least the cooling off period of crossing the room before blowing his brains out in misery over his late wife's absence.

For a while he just sat there, on the bed but with his feet on the wood floor in the slippers, looking through the yellowish glow of the bedside lamp, staring at the wall beyond which was the kitchen where the noises had seemed to come from.

Nothing.

Nothing.

Nothing.

Goddamnit, he thought, and stepped out of his slippers and slid under the covers again, got comfy, and a scraping sound, like a chair being pushed back, sat him up again. Then he was in his slippers and across the room and digging that .38 out from under some of his Jean's clothes that he hadn't been able to bring himself yet to get rid of.

He prowled the condo.

Slow, methodical, turning on lights as he went. Gun gripped in his right hand, like a cop in black silk pajamas and slippers, Vernon checked everywhere, even the stupid places—under tables, in closets, in back of the couch, behind the recliner. Periodically he would stand and listen and hear nothing but his heartbeat and the hum of kitchen appliances.

And in the kitchen, he found something that disturbed him—the double glass doors onto the deck weren't locked. He didn't remember locking them, but he also didn't remember *not* locking them. Someone could have had got in.

But no one was here now. He was sure of that. He'd checked the premises as thoroughly as a security guard at a nuclear power plant.

Maybe someone had got in, realized Vernon was there and been scared away. But why wouldn't a thief expect the condo owner to be home? And if the guy had done any casing of the joint, as they said in the movies, wouldn't it be obvious an old guy lived here? Seventy-five-the-hell-years old? Or had a home invader gotten in while Vernon was away, at the movie, and at Jessica's apartment cheating on his dead wife? (That was exactly how his brain told it to him and it made him laugh, bitterly.) And then after Vernon got home, the invader slipped out and bumped into something doing so? Maybe?

Well, he had searched the place thoroughly and no one was here. If a burglar had been here and gone, and looted him in any way, he would conduct an inventory tomorrow and see what was missing and call the police. What the hell—he was well-insured, wasn't he?

Of course, he immediately locked the glass doors to the deck, and took one last, lingering pass around the condo just to make sure, shutting the lights back off as he went. In the bedroom, he compromised on the .38, leaving it atop the dresser but not tucking it away in a bunch of Jean's clothes. By the time he was out of his slippers and under the covers, he felt confident. A little unsettled, sure.

Sleep was just taking over when a scuttling sound jerked him upright.

Good lord, something was *under* him!

Moving under the bed, like a giant goddamn crab! The moon was coming in through filmy curtains onto the river and Vernon sat on the bed with his legs far apart now, as if making room for whatever was under there.

Was it an animal?

If so, could he make it back to the dresser and the revolver before whatever it was had him?

But what was *it?*

Then the moon slid under a cloud and the thing beneath the bed scurried out from under, and Vernon still couldn't make it out; it was as if some giant turtle or clam with limbs were moving across the parquet wood floor, scratching. Then the thing was out of sight again, just beyond the foot of the bed.

Vernon threw the covers off and was about to run, to get himself somewhere, anywhere else, when the dark form came clambering up onto the bed and clawing at the bottom sheet and coming right at him, *on* him, up from between his legs and, my God, it had arms and hands, and those hands were climbing Vernon's torso like a ladder, forcing him back down, and then a face was staring right at him, nose to nose, a grotesque, twisted thing framed in a matted unruly mop, eyes glittering, yellow teeth bared and uneven, creased like a simian but no ape, no monkey, something worse.

And Vernon grabbed at him—this was no monster, it was a man! And a doctor knew how to hurt people, so he rallied himself and grabbed at this man, but then the turtle-shell form he'd seen reminded him that there was no man down there to grab, that this was *half* a man.

The doctor screamed, and the half-man grabbed the other pillow and pressed it into the screamer's face and held it down and held it and held it until Vernon wasn't struggling anymore—smothered to death in a pillow still redolent with his late wife's perfume.

CHAPTER 2

Blake Cutter, chief of police of Peachtree Heights, Georgia, pulled his personal vehicle, a steel-gray Dodge Challenger, through the gate of the fieldstone walled-in compound of Dr. Roy Ryan's residence and clinic.

A gravel drive cut through the slightly overgrown lawn and widened into an apron around a large, rambling wooden two-story home dating to the turn of the century. A pair of outlying buildings on either side of the house represented Dr. Ryan's office in a cement-block building and a similar structure given over to equipment used for tending to the large yard. It was well known that the late Dr. Raymond Ryan, Roy's father, had allowed Depression-era patients who were able-bodied but not able to pay his fee to instead work at maintaining the yard and its shrubbery.

That old-fashioned tradition was eventually replaced by Roy and his brother and sister taking over the yard work when they were of high school age. Roy's grown siblings lived out of state, and were also doctors—of medicine and archeology respectively. But after their father died of a heart attack earlier this year, it was Roy who returned to be in-house gardener and physician. One day, perhaps, his boy Richie would take over the lawn work.

Perhaps.

Cutter knew ten year-old Richie was a Special Needs kid, but pleasant and seemingly sharper than most in his category. Just exactly what Richie was capable of, Cutter wasn't sure—the chief was friendly with Roy Ryan but not close to the man, who had only moved back home upon the elder Ryan's passing last year, taking over both the family home and his late dad's practice, bringing his son along...but not his wife.

The old homestead needed work, probably more than one man—particularly a busy family practitioner—could manage. But Cutter felt confident Roy was up to both tasks. And everyone in town knew the young Dr. Ryan had walked away from a high-paying practice in Atlanta to return to his roots in Peachtree Heights.

Cutter himself was not a native of the place. He was a Georgia boy, all right, if a man of fifty might be termed a "boy," having grown up in Atlanta where he lived until his football scholarship to Georgia Tech was interrupted by Pearl Harbor. After the war, Cutter had married a New York girl he'd met at the USO there, and wound up with a career in law enforcement. He'd been a captain of homicide when he retired last year, after which he landed this job as chief of police in Peachtree Heights, a town of about 15,000 close to Atlanta but not quite a suburb.

Cutter's ex-wife Dorrie still lived in the Coca Cola capitol. They were on friendly terms and he was working at getting her back—she hadn't remarried, which was a good sign, and his two grown kids (Mary and Bill) were on his side. Dorrie hated his profession, the danger, the long hours, and considered her husband a workaholic.

He'd hoped to prove her wrong with his new job, trading New York for a classic American small town, and so far it had been easier, more administrative than anything. He'd taken over from a chief tossed out on corruption charges that had impacted the ten-man force. Cutter replaced most of them with other recent NYPD retirees, assembling a great damn staff he could be proud of. His captain, Leon Jackson, was his solid right hand, although after getting a look at the little town, Leon had asked, "Where are the damn peach trees?"

"They were all killed by a fungus in 1857, Leon."

"And what's 'heights' about it? I don't see any damn hills."

"Lots of towns flatter than a pancake use 'Heights,' Leon—way back when, it attracted settlers. *You* settled here, didn't you?"

Leon made a big bearded face. "I came for the peaches, boss, but so far it's the pits."

Cutter smiled at the thought of that, but knew Leon was settling in just fine.

Four cars were pulled in near the porch—next to each other were a Chevy sedan, dark blue with medical license plates, and a pink Oldsmobile Toronado that screamed money...and a visit from Mrs. Ryan. She was not quite the doc's ex yet—they were separated—but word around town said divorce was inevitable.

The other two vehicles were Peachtree Heights PD patrol cars, "Serve and Protect" black-and-whites. Each had brought two officers who could be seen right now, walking the periphery, across the lawn, around the outbuildings, along the walls. One might have thought this was a place under siege.

One might not have been entirely wrong.

The chief stepped from the Dodge into the cold, crisp night and took off his tan Stetson, surveying the scene.

He wore a black PD windbreaker and white shirt-and-tie with chinos, a Smith & Wesson Model 39 nine millimeter on his hip. The rangy six-footer had only a hint of paunch, his craggy western lawman's face topped by short, ragged brown hair going white. He had blue eyes on loan from Paul Newman and no idea how impressive he looked. Or at least he wasn't about to admit it.

He nodded at the nearest of his men, patrolling the grounds, got a nod back, and climbed the four steps to the slightly saggy porch. His knock was answered by Dr. Roy himself, slender but sturdy-looking in a sports coat and Polo and jeans, brown hair cut short, face a handsome, friendly oval, but his dark blue eyes were almost lost under his furrowed brow.

"You all right, Doc?"

Ryan whispered, "I've been better. Helen is here. Her hair's on fire about all this."

Cutter grunted a laugh. "Maybe you need the fire department not the police."

The dark blue eyes showed themselves. "Oh, I *need* the police. I think you know that, Chief."

Ryan stepped to one side and Cutter went in. He'd been here several times, yet the room was always something of a surprise—the ceiling rose to the full two-stories, with a central open staircase curving to a half upper floor of bedrooms while this chamber seemed like maybe a wall had been torn from between the living room and parlor of what was already a spacious house.

At left was a brick fireplace with an oil painting of Ryan's late parents above it, when they were the age Roy and Helen were now, smiling from eternity. A once elegant couch faced the fire, waiting patiently for re-upholstery. Here and there were corners with lamps and chairs for reading, and several sitting areas with chairs and two-seater sofas, making many rooms of this one.

An at once magnificent and shabby space, this was a living room designed, unlike most, for actual living. Over at right was a sort of library with lots of books, both medical and popular fiction; but also on the built-in shelves were the modern intrusions of a television and a hi-fi system.

The boy, Richie, was sitting on the floor in his blue and red Superman pajamas, looking up at the TV resting on an adult's eye-level shelf. He glanced at Cutter coming in, smiled, and waved; the chief waved back and the boy returned to *The Amazing Spider-Man* on the tube.

Helen was sitting on that sofa in front of the fireplace, where flames were licking and snapping—the night was chill enough for that. She rose as Cutter entered, a stunning woman in her early thirties, almost as tall as her husband, shapely and just tanned enough, with eyes as blue as Cutter's own and long blonde hair brushing the shoulders of a long-sleeved second skin of a black top and bell-bottom jeans. She wore sandals, a rich hippie.

She looked pissed.

Clearly Cutter had entered mid-argument.

She came over quickly and planted herself before him and said, "You're Chief Cutter, I take it?"

"I am."

"These are your men, walking the grounds?"

"They are. I take it you're Mrs. Ryan."

"For the moment. Are you a part of this?"

"A part of what, ma'am?"

She frowned; oddly, she was just as beautiful doing so, nothing at all ugly about her but her tone. "Spare me the *Dragnet* routine. I came down here in good faith, for a reasonable discussion with Roy about arranging shared custody of our son Richard, and what do I find? This...this *circus*."

Roy, at Cutter's side and facing the angry woman, bit

the words off: "You can't really imagine I would, that I *could* enlist the entire Peachtree Heights police department just to hang onto Richie for a few days while I, what? Cook up some evil plan with a small-town lawyer to go up against your father's fleet of big-city, big-shot attorneys?"

"You did all right for yourself before!" she said, shaking a fist.

Whoa, Cutter thought. He didn't know the specifics, just that somehow Dr. Roy had won full custody of his son. Rumor around Peachtree Heights was that the doc's wife must be wild or something. Maybe on drugs or running around with men. Or, worse, women!

Mad as a wet hen though she might be, however, this was obviously no drug addict, and who she was or wasn't having sex with was beside the point—her love for her son was clear by the depth of her rage.

Cutter needed to settle this shit down.

"Mrs. Ryan...or would you prefer 'Helen'? I'm Blake. I'm really not the enemy, and I assure you this is *not* some crazy scheme to get the best of you in your custody battle. Could you and Mr. Ryan just...sit down for a moment, and let me fill you both in?"

The woman took a deep breath and let it out. She swallowed. Nodded. "Yes. Certainly. And 'Helen' is fine...Blake."

Ryan and his estranged wife deposited themselves on the sofa, leaving a cushion's worth of space between them. Placing his Stetson and windbreaker on a nearby chair, Cutter put himself opposite that empty cushion with the warmth of the fire behind him. The real heat was coming from Mrs. Ryan, who watched him with skeptical tolerance. Flames reflected and danced on the faces of both wife and husband, as if God or anyway some god were laughing at them.

Cutter began: "Helen, I take it you're aware of what's happened in and around Peachtree Heights over the past month and a half?"

Helen nodded. "Three retired doctors have died. Accidental deaths in two cases, natural causes in the other."

Cutter nodded, slowly, saying, "Died, yes. But not accidents, and *not* of natural causes."

She frowned. "You were asked by reporters in Atlanta whether these were murders and your reply was, I believe, 'no comment.'"

Cutter shrugged. "That was accurately reported. But 'no comment' and 'no' are two very different responses. We are not anxious to advertise it, just yet...but these *are* looking like murders."

She did not seem impressed.

Her husband, however, was sitting forward, eyes narrowed and alert. "Including that obstetrician? Vernon Petersen?"

Again Cutter nodded. "His is the most obvious murder, but our medical examiner has only just confirmed the cause of death. Suffocation. Indications are Dr. Petersen was smothered with a pillow."

Now Helen's head cocked and an eyebrow raised. "What about the other two?"

"Dr. Samuel Carter, pediatric surgeon, fell down the stairs. Hard to prove that one's a murder, but the carpeted stairs do tell a story of sorts—for it to be an accidental death, Carter would've had to miss the first three steps entirely, based upon where blood and broken teeth were found, indicating he first hit his head half-way down before tumbling the rest of the way and breaking his neck."

That made Helen wince.

"As for Dr. Lee Meyer," Cutter said, "he drowned, all

right. And was washed ashore. But his shoulders were bruised, as if he'd been held under water."

"Are these injuries," Helen asked, "absolute proof of murder and not accident?"

"No," Cutter admitted. "Carter could have missed the first step and Meyer might have been bruised by objects in the water. But Petersen's death seals it. It's absolutely suffocation."

Helen's eyes were slits now. "How can you know that for certain?"

But it was her husband who answered: "Petechial hemorrhaging."

Cutter clarified: "Red or purple splotches in the eyes, face, neck. Your husband showed you the note?"

She twitched a frown. "Yes. Just before you got here. But...nothing."

Ryan said, "She thought I was lying. That I made it up! Can you believe this bullshit?"

Cutter held up a gentling hand. He went to his windbreaker and got out the plastic-sheathed note and came over and handed the missive to her.

She read it.

Cutter knew what it said, in cut-out letters from area newspapers and national magazines: NOT JUST A DOCTOR THIS TIME. FIRST THE BOY. THIS IN PAYMENT FOR WHAT THEY DID TO ME.

"How..." She swallowed, thrust the plastic-encased note back to Cutter. "...how do we know an unsigned piece of garbage like that isn't just...just a goddamn *prank?*"

Cutter flipped a hand. "To what end?"

She had no answer to that, but asked pointedly, "Why wasn't I told about that vile note sooner?"

"It showed up in your husband's mailbox today. We

take it to mean it's a deranged individual with one hell of a grudge against doctors."

"Doctors in general?" Helen asked. "Or specific doctors?"

Ryan said, "She has a point. Two of the victims are pediatricians. The one last week, an obstetrician. All child-oriented physicians. But I'm a general practitioner. A family doctor."

"Family doctors," Helen said, her voice different now, "look after kids. What do you think, Blake?"

"Frankly I'm not sure," Cutter admitted. Her using his first name was a good sign—she was finally buying in. "But right now we're checking the cases histories in the files of the three dead doctors and looking for a tie-up, any connection at all." To Roy, he said, "We'd like to add you into the mix, Dr. Ryan."

"Anything you need," he said.

Helen drew in another big breath and let it out. "I suppose I should thank you, Chief Cutter." The informality of "Blake" was gone suddenly. "And even you, Roy...because you make my case better than I ever could. Our son is much better off in *my* custody now, for obvious reasons."

Ryan began, "Helen, that's *not* the way to—"

Cutter cut in. "Mrs. Ryan...upon my recommendation, no judge in this state would release your boy from here—for one thing, it might void the current custody agreement."

"I'll sign off on that!" Helen blurted. "I'm only thinking of Richard's safety."

"If you lived out of state," Cutter said calmly, "perhaps Richard would be safer with you. But you are in Atlanta, apparently well within the reach of this madman, I'm afraid."

She was shaking her head, the blonde hair flying.

"Peachtree Heights is a small town, Chief Cutter—you have a minuscule force. The Atlanta police are entirely more qualified to—"

Cutter cut in again. "I am a former NYPD captain and I've assembled an elite, educated, well-trained and experienced team. Please don't underestimate our capabilities. But even granting some of your concerns, a judge will understand the situation completely. This compound, walled-in as it is, and with our ability to patrol and guard here, make protecting your son an achievable priority. And if necessary, we have relationships with the Atlanta PD and the various suburban agencies and can draw support from those circles."

She was sitting up straight now. "And, what? I'm supposed to stay out of this until you say otherwise?"

"I'm afraid you don't have any choice, Mrs. Ryan. Not unless you want to expose your son to the possibility of extreme danger."

"I could fight it," she said tightly. "My father..."

"Your father has money," Cutter said, "and connections. No doubt about it. If that's the way you want to go, it's your prerogative."

Ryan said, with some acid in it, "For all his wealth and power, darling, your daddy and his legal fleet weren't able to take Richie away from me before. You said so yourself."

"Bastard!"

"Bitch."

Cutter said, "May I make a suggestion? You have an impressionable young man across the room there, watching TV, who I'm sure loves you both and would not benefit from hearing language like that, or seeing two people he loves going at each other's throats."

Both Mr. and Mrs. Ryan hung their heads.

Roy said, "You're right." He looked at her across the

endless divide of a single couch cushion. "Honey...I'm sorry. But for now, Richie's better off here."

She looked sharply at him. "Then *I'm* staying right here. With my son. Until this situation *is* resolved. If he's safe here, I'm safe here."

Her husband seemed amused. "You're comfortable, being under the same roof with me?"

"Oh, you'll be quite safe from me, and I from you. I'm not about to abrogate our separation agreement, Roy. There are plenty of extra bedrooms here and, with so many police patrolling, plenty of prying eyes to keep everybody honest. And I'm sure any judge will understand my desire to be with my son in these circumstances....don't you agree, Chief Cutter?"

Cutter, arms folded, grinned at the pair. "I'm quite sure any judge would heartily agree, Mrs. Ryan." He went over and plucked his windbreaker from the chair and climbed into the jacket. "For now we'll have four men outside the place, round the clock. We'll keeps tabs on the phone calls coming in. This character with his newspaper-clipping note doesn't seem like the telephone type, but you never know."

As Cutter put on his Stetson, Ryan rose. "You need to put somebody on the phone here in the house, Blake?"

Cutter shook his head. "We can set that up with the phone company." He got a card out of his breast pocket and a pen from his jacket, jotted his home number down. "If you can't get me at the PD, call me there. Any hour of the day or night. You have a gun, Roy?"

"No. Not in a house with...a young boy."

"I understand that concern. But you may want to reconsider in these circumstances. Can you line up other docs to fill in with your patients? I want to keep that gate closed with as little coming and going as possible. You got enough food on hand to stay in for a while?"

Ryan nodded, then walked the chief to the door and asked him, "What should I tell the medics filling in for me?"

"Say you've got the flu."

"That typically doesn't last longer than a couple of weeks."

Cutter gave Ryan a hard look. "Let's hope that's more time than we need."

CHAPTER 3

Roy Ryan shut the door behind Chief Cutter and turned, looking across the big open room divided by the curving stairway, a space welcoming if a bit shabby, past the cozy areas and occasional windows letting in moonlight. His son was off to the right watching a cheesy live-action super-hero on TV; on the couch his estranged wife sat facing the dancing orange and blue of the fireplace flames. She fit in here, a warm woman despite her cold upbringing, a beautiful specimen of the female sex whose features had delicacy but also strength, her blonde hair glowing in the firelight.

He couldn't help himself—he still loved her. But she had let him down—putting her controlling old man before the needs of their little family, and the son who embarrassed that other, larger family, one of Atlanta's most powerful and socially prominent.

Helen's father, Alexander Parsons, was the second-generation head of Georgia National, the USA's leading manufacturer and marketer of tissue, pulp, packaging and building products. They made everything from toilet paper to paper cups, from office supplies to drywall.

Also, a lot of money—her father's favorite paper product, one of the few he did not himself directly manufacture.

Among the family's supposedly public-spirited (and tax write-off) enterprises was a clinic in Atlanta where Roy had been set up with a practice whose patients were only the "right" kind of people. When Roy tried to expand to include a free clinic for, well, the "wrong" kind of people (in Helen's father's eyes) that had caused a nasty breach.

But it still hadn't been enough to make Roy break away. That took the Parsons family's increasingly short-sighted attitude about Richie, who they bounced from one expert to another and had privately tutored, denying the boy any access to other kids his age.

The back-breaking straw had been their decision to have the child institutionalized, which Helen had gone along with. Roy considered his wife's compliance a betrayal of both himself and their son, leading to their separation, and in turn to the custody battle. Fortunately, a judge—unimpressed with the Parsons political power and outraged by a child diagnosed only marginally as "special needs" being institutionalized—gave Roy custody to the child with only limited visitation rights to Helen.

He crossed the room and joined her on the couch, maintaining that unpassable border of a center cushion. Her chin bobbed up almost imperceptibly, the blue eyes not leaving the flickering flames, a mild acknowledgment of his presence beside her. Almost beside her.

"I love my son," she said quietly.

"I know you do."

"I just wanted...*want*...what's best for him." Now she looked at him. "You left him to me. To my care. But he didn't need a mother."

"Of course he did."

Her full lips turned into two tight lines. "That's not what I mean. He needed *you*, a father, and you were too busy trying to get that stupid free clinic up and running for...for *whoever*...and didn't give Richard the attention he needs."

He paused, and when he spoke again his voice was soft. "You're not wrong. I'm trying to make up for it now."

Her eyebrows lifted. "Better late than never?"

His voice came back, not soft: "Would it have been so hard for you to set up your precious art studio at home? And be with him? A boy like that needed *us*, not a nanny, not shrinks and 'developmental' experts. He's not a genius, okay, but so what? I see him as a normal boy."

She lowered her head and her eyes bore into him like a bull considering a matador. "And your idea of 'normal' is to put him in public school, with their 'special education' classes...our son, taking the 'short bus'!" She shuddered, hugged her arms to herself, as if the fire wasn't enough. "It's just your lazy way of keeping him off your hands while you see your precious patients."

"That's how you look at me, is it? Tonight, for example. You really thought I was capable of staging, of faking, some threat to Richie just to buy some time in your father's next legal assault on my son and me?"

She shook her head, sighing. "Why not? You're capable of anything, Roy. You talk a good game, but really? The only thing you've ever thought of is yourself."

"Just because I busted my ass working—"

Her eyes and nostrils flared. "Working to help who? Not us. You had to be some bleeding heart. Free clinic! You just did that to stick a finger in Daddy's eye!"

Roy leaned across the cushion divide. "Wasn't it bad

enough that I lowered myself to taking a handout from your father—"

"Handout!" Her eyes showed white all round. "Running a damn *clinic* was a *handout?*"

"Putting me in charge, right out of medical school? Damn well told! So the least I could do was give something back—"

Her eyes narrowed now. "You didn't have anything to give back that my family didn't *give* you in the first place."

She returned her eyes to the fire, arms still folded.

In every discussion like this, between a husband and wife, one of two things must happen: somebody walks out of the room; or somebody changes the subject. Roy decided to change the subject.

"If you're going to stay here for a while," he said, "you'll need to have some things sent up from Atlanta. Till then, the bathroom near the south guest room has enough toiletries for you to get by."

She shook her head, the blonde hair bouncing on her shoulders just a little. "Not necessary. I have an overnight bag in the car."

He eyed her warily. "You were already figuring for an overnight stay?"

A shrug. "I didn't know how long this...negotiation was going to take."

He frowned, genuinely confused. "*What* negotiation?"

Another shrug. "Getting you to come to your senses and share custody."

He huffed a laugh. "What did you have in mind, a seduction job?"

Her chin crinkled, but then irritation turned into amusement, despite herself.

"You *wish.*" She shifted on her couch cushion. "I think we've explored this thoroughly enough for now. I have a motel reservation to cancel. And we have a lot of talking to do, starting tomorrow. This isn't over—it's just beginning."

"Hell," he said, lifting a shoulder and setting it back down. "You're welcome to stay as long as you want."

A voice between them, high-pitched but male, said, "Are you *really* staying, Mom?"

Peeking over the center of the couch from in back of them was the bright-eyed face of ten year-old Richard Ryan. That he looked so much like Helen's father was a bitter irony they'd both long since gotten past.

"I'm staying," she confirmed. "Have you been listening long, honey?"

"No. What's a suh-*duck*-shun job?"

His parents looked at each other.

"If *Spider-man*'s over," Roy said, ignoring the question, "you should get up to your room, and get yourself in bed."

"Who's gonna tuck me in? Maybe Mom?"

"Sure," she said. "Go on up and brush your teeth and climb under the covers. I'll be right up."

Richie did neither of those things, instead scrambling around to plant himself between them on the couch. The boy looked at his mother like Christmas was coming, and soon. "If you're staying? Can we go on the rides at the park? Maybe go on the pond in a boat? Can *I* row?"

"Well..." she started.

"Maybe the park in a few days," Roy finished for her. "For now we have to stay inside."

The boy frowned. "Because you're sick?"

"What makes you think I'm sick, son?"

"You have the flu, don't you?"

How long had *the boy been listening?*

"Well, I *am* sick..." Roy began.

"I'll say," Helen muttered.

"...but it's not serious. We're just going to stay in, here at the house, till we're sure you and Mom haven't caught this bug."

"Like a quarantine," the boy said.

His parents exchanged looks again—this kid, so under-estimated, came up with the damnedest words sometimes.

"Like that," Roy said.

Richie frowned, curious. "Is that why those policemen are out walking around?"

"Uh, yeah. That's right."

The boy's head tilted to one side. "Is that for keeping somebody from getting in? Or for us getting out?"

"They're just protecting us."

He winced in thought. "What about school?"

"I'll let your principal know. You'll do homework here."

Richie jerked a thumb toward his mother. "Is Mom staying to be your nurse?"

She mouthed *You wish* at Roy, who said, "If we need her to. But mostly she'll just be Mom. You two can catch up—you haven't spent much time together lately."

"I know!" Richie turned to her. "Can we play games?"

"Sure," Helen said.

"Like Operation? I think it's funny when the tweezers make it buzz."

"Me, too," Roy said. "But real operations aren't so funny."

"I know! You're a *real* doctor. This is just pretend."

"Right."

"I'm going to be a doctor someday. I still have what you gave me! That old stethoscope."

Another mouthful the kid managed, and remembered.

The boy was saying, "I'm gonna get it out and be *your* doctor, Dad!"

He ruffled the boy's hair. "Why not? But for now, doctor's orders are Richard Thomas Ryan needs to get himself to bed. Mom will be up soon."

"And you, too?"

"Sure."

The boy scrambled away and went up the stairs— slow and careful, as he'd been taught, then scrambling again when he reached the top.

"Why do you encourage him?" Helen asked. Suddenly she seemed on the verge of tears.

"What are you talking about?"

"Telling a boy like Richard he can be a doctor some-day. What is *wrong* with you?"

"What's the harm? So he has a vivid imagination—so what? I think it's a good sign—even your developmental jerks say so. Right now he wants to be a doctor—last week it was Batman, next week it'll be one of these cops walking the grounds."

She was shaking her head. "I don't agree that his imagination is a good thing. You let him watch too much unsupervised TV. Do you want him to jump off the roof in his Superman pajamas? And it's cruel of you."

"What is?"

"Putting it in his head he could be grow up to be a doctor."

Roy rolled his eyes. "Oh, for Pete's sake. Suppose he *does* develop an actual interest in medicine—he's so much brighter than your 'experts' indicate. Can't you see how he's blossoming?"

"He's more like a six-year-old than almost eleven."

"But a *normal* six-year-old. And even if he's not a genius, he could be a male nurse or maybe an orderly. I mean, his vocabulary—'quarantine'? How about stethoscope'? How many kids his age with their high IQs know *that* one?"

She sighed. "It's just dangerous, getting his hopes up. You're his hero, Roy. He sees you and wants to be a doctor. It's cruel."

Glass shattered and an object came flying through the picture window to the left of the fireplace, knocking a lamp off a table, sailing in like a terrible bird that had caught fire. Helen gasped and Roy, momentarily stunned, realized what he was looking at, as it spun on the wood floor like a deadly top spitting flames—a bottle of fluid, its cloth wick already lit.

"Get away and down!" he yelled at his wife, and bolted to the bottle and grabbed it and thrust it back out through the jagged-toothed aperture in the window. The burning bottle hit the lawn and exploded in a burst of flame that illuminated something scurrying away, something...

....human?

A broad-shouldered creature in black on no discernible legs, its long simian-like arms outstretched, was moving quickly, though the motion was more side to side than forward, and yet in a few eyeblinks he was at the fieldstone wall, climbing it as quickly as a squirrel up the side of a brick building and...

Gone.

Roy yanked off his sports coat and smothered the flames the burning bottle had deposited on the wooden floor. Outside, the fire was ebbing but still vivid in the night and three cops were rushing to where the Molotov cocktail had landed after Roy lobbed it, the trio apparently not having seen the fleeing...*man?*...who had obviously hurled the makeshift bomb in the first place. A fourth cop joined them, having availed himself of a fire extinguisher and got to work putting out the flames.

Roy went back to Helen and said to her, "It's all right. Check on Richie," and got a long-stemmed flashlight from a drawer before going out to join the four officers.

Leon Jackson, a big trimly bearded African-American officer who the chief had left in charge, approached as Roy exited the house and ran down the steps off the porch.

"Did you see it?" Roy asked, almost yelling, though the only sounds were the steamy noise of the fire extinguisher and the snap of the dying flames. "Did any of your men see it?"

"*It?*"

Roy nodded several times, fast. "If it was a man, it was the damnedest man I ever saw. I think he was in a black sweater, maybe a cap—he went over the wall...there."

Roy pointed.

Jackson trotted over and sent two of his men out to check the other side of the wall, where a strip of grass bordered trees, then returned to the doctor.

"It was more like...*half* a man," Roy said. "But he had legs...or anyway feet, or...."

Jackson put a hand on Roy's shoulder. "It's okay, doctor. Just tell me what you saw."

Roy did, but could add nothing to what he'd already shared, other than, "He scrambled up that wall like a damn monkey. So fast. So goddamn *fast*....."

Gently, hand still on Roy's shoulder, Jackson said, "Now, come on, doctor. You do better than that. What did he look like?"

"I only got a glimpse."

"Try. You're a medical man, now. Amputee? Dwarf? Try."

Roy shook his head. "You'd need Dr. Frankenstein for

the right medical opinion on this one. Get Chief Cutter out here, would you?"

"You bet."

"*Sergeant Jackson!*"

The cry came from one of the other cops stepping just inside the gate, which they'd opened to check out the perimeter. Jackson jogged over to the officer and Roy followed.

The cop, a skinny guy in his forties who wore an alarmed expression, had a flashlight, too. "You need to see this, Sergeant."

Roy followed Jackson taking the other officer's lead, flashlight beams cutting the night. Another cop with a flashlight was already illuminating footprints in soft ground—it had rained a few days ago—trailing into the nearby trees.

The footprints were those of a large man—a barefoot man.

"What the hell," Jackson said to nobody in particular, "are we looking at?"

"He doesn't have much of a stride," the skinny officer said.

Roy said, "Why would he? He's only about three feet tall."

All the cops looked at him like he was crazy. Which was exactly how Roy felt.

Before long Roy was back inside, where the fire on the floor was out, the charred sports coat cast aside, an officer taking Polaroid pictures of the blackened, glass-scattered area. Helen was over on the couch sitting next to Richie, who was snuggled against her in his pjs. A lot of lights had been turned on. The boy straightened and smiled as his father approached, then the child's expression tightened like a fist.

"What the hell was that, Dad?"

"Language," his mother said, without much conviction.

"Dad says that all the time," the boy said defensively, then words came tumbling from him: "I saw the fire from my window, Dad. And those cops standing around it like a marshmallow roast. What the...heck's going on?"

"Is that all you saw?" Roy said, and sat next to them.

"That's all."

"Probably some kids. Halloween."

"Dad, Halloween's two weeks from now."

Roy smiled, shrugged. "Sometimes big kids get an early start."

Richie shook his head. "Kids shouldn't play with fire, even if they are big."

"No, they shouldn't. You better scoot upstairs, son."

The boy turned to his mother. "Tuck me in again?"

She smiled, took his hand. "You bet."

"See you in the morning, Dad!"

The officer with the camera had just left when Helen came down. Wind was whistling tunelessly through the open window. Roy stood looking at the scorched floor.

She slipped her arm in her husband's, looking toward the jagged remains of the picture window. "We'll need to board that up tomorrow."

"I'll take care of it tonight." He kicked at the shards on the floor. "Guess you believe me now. Unless you think I really know how to put on a show."

"I believe you." Her eyes were on the broken window. "You saw something out there. What did you see?"

He didn't answer at first. Instead he led her back to the couch and they sat again. No cushion between them now. He told her as best he could.

She shivered, held onto his arm again. "Sounds like something out of *King Kong*."

"More like *Murders in the Rue Morgue*."

They just sat there for a while, the fire dwindling, at once comforting and yet a reminder of the more unpleasant flames that had come sailing through the window not long ago.

Finally Roy said, "What happened to us, baby?"

"Maybe...maybe there wasn't *enough* 'us.' Just you and your practice and your idealism. And me and my artwork and the gallery."

Her father had set her up with an art gallery in Atlanta's Little Five points area of quirky shops and boutiques. She was not an arty type, though—she did lovely landscapes that the tourists bought. She was good. He was proud of her for that.

He walked her out to the Toronado and they collected her suitcase.

"If we're going to be trapped in here for a few days," Roy said, as they headed back in, "maybe we can work some things out. Without any lawyers."

"Without my father?"

"Without your father."

"About Richard."

"About Richie."

He escorted her to the foot of the stairs and she started up without him, then turned and said, "Roy, you should know that I don't have any desire to play the little woman to a small-town doctor."

"I suppose you'd like it better if I had a private practice in Buckhead."

"Yes. I would."

And she went up to bed.

As he hammered the boards in place over the busted-out window, he hoped he was disturbing her rest.

CHAPTER 4

The morning was overcast as Chief Blake Cutter joined Dr. Roy Ryan in the yard where Sgt. Jackson was kneeling as he made moulage casts of more footprints left by last night's visitor.

Hands on hips, Cutter—who didn't know what the hell to make of the large feet with the extended, gripping toes the prints suggested—said, "Well, what exactly *did* you see, Doctor?"

As Ryan watched Jackson work, he said, "Just what I told you. A low-to-the-ground shape in black, like the top half of a man, broad shoulders, long arms, fingers apart, as if about to...clutch or grab or climb. His movement was as much side to side as forward, yet he moved remarkably fast."

"A dwarf, possibly?"

Ryan shrugged. "Maybe so, but I couldn't make out any legs."

Cutter's eyebrows raised as he pointed to a print in the damp earth. "Well, he obviously has feet. I guess we can safely deduce he has legs."

With a hint of dry sarcasm, Ryan said, "You're the

detective....It's muggy out here. Hope the sun burns this off." He turned to the chief. "How about some coffee? I made some breakfast, if you like grits."

"No thanks. I'm not *that* Southern. But I'll take you up on that coffee."

In the spacious old-fashioned dark-wood kitchen off the big open living room, Helen Ryan—in a light yellow blouse and orange slacks and open-toed sandals—was seated at the table with a cup of coffee, a dish of grits and some toast. The lovely young woman, with her blonde shoulder-brushing hair and expertly applied make-up, rose and smiled politely at the chief, exchanging nods with him, and offered to get him coffee. Even casually dressed, the doctor's wife seemed like the hostess at some elegant cocktail party.

"Thanks, Helen," Cutter said. "Black."

Ryan said, "For me too, please."

She delivered on those requests and joined her husband and their official guest at the old cherry-wood table with the nicks and gouges of thousands of breakfasts. "No further incidents last night?"

Cutter shook his head. "None, fortunately. But *unfortunately* no one but Mr. Ryan here got any kind of look at your guest."

"Not *any* of your four officers?"

"Nothing useful."

Her look was coolly judgmental. "Yet despite those four officers, our intruder made it over the wall, hurled a burning missile, and made his way back over the wall and into the night?"

Cutter sipped his coffee. "Despite that, yes. But we've had presidents in this country killed surrounded by Secret Service security. The attacker always has a certain advantage in these situations."

Helen raised her eyebrows. "That's hardly a reassuring point of view."

The chief tried to soften things with a smile. "Sorry. But before, having men posted was a precaution. Now, we're on the alert."

The two men resumed what appeared to be a conversation they were in the middle of.

Cutter asked, "Could your caller have been an amputee?"

Ryan smirked at that. "With feet?"

"Obviously there are prosthetic limbs available..."

"Which just as obviously would make him taller than the less-than-four-foot creature I saw. And what kind of prosthetic limb would leave *those* kind of footprints?"

Cutter sighed. "None I can imagine."

Helen frowned at her husband. "You make it sound like something from a horror film—a 'creature.' This must be a person, a little person most likely." To Cutter she said, "I could try to draw a sketch for you, unless you already have a police artist available."

"We don't. You're an artist, Mrs. Ryan?"

"'Helen,' remember? Yes. I have a gallery in Buckhead, and a degree from UGA."

Nodding, Cutter said, "That's an excellent suggestion and a good offer. A little department like ours doesn't have a sketch artist on staff, and this saves me begging Atlanta to send one down."

They moved into the living room and onto the couch, the fireplace unlighted this time of day. Helen sat between the two men, her husband in a gray polo and darker gray slacks, Cutter in his usual short-sleeve white shirt with tie and chinos. The chief's Stetson and black windbreaker were on a nearby chair as if keeping guard over the Rorschach blot of scorched wood on the floor from last night's Molotov cocktail.

The sketch came quickly and Ryan identified it as an

accurate representation of what he'd seen. But as that had been a rear view of their unwanted visitor, its helpfulness was limited, though the chief was impressed with the artistic skill of his hostess.

"So if, as you say, he wore a sweater or jacket," Cutter said to Ryan, "that could have ridden down over legs, however stubby, giving the impression of a head and torso moving *minus* legs."

"A dwarf, then," Ryan said.

The chief shrugged. "That's the only answer I can come up with. But most little people aren't broad-shouldered, long-armed and, at the same time, remarkably agile."

"Little or not," Helen said, "they are first and foremost people, good and bad and in-between like the rest of us. Surely if there are criminals among them, that would be on the books. Small stature might prove useful in home invasions, wouldn't it?"

Cutter nodded. "That's a good point, and we'll run checks. But this isn't a standard-issue criminal—it would appear to be a madman. What the FBI these days is calling a serial killer."

Helen said, "With a grudge against doctors."

The chief again nodded. "As you suggested last night, possibly doctors whose patients include, or are exclusively, children. And if we can find a specific link between the three victims, a genuine tie-up, we would have a real shot at figuring what's going on here...and stopping this madman."

Helen's eyes moved past Cutter and she raised "shush" fingers to her lips. "Here comes Richard...."

The boy, in a white and navy-blue-striped short-sleeve shirt and denims and tennies, trotted in, smiling. A stethoscope was around the child's neck—Cutter had no idea what *that* was about....

"Morning, Dad," Richie said, beaming. "Morning, Mom. Morning, Chief Cutter."

Everybody said hello to the polite child.

"Did I miss breakfast?" he asked.

His mother assured him he hadn't and the little group returned to the kitchen, where Richie helped himself to a bowl of grits. His mother got him a glass of milk and the boy unceremoniously joined them at the table, between his mom and dad.

"Dad makes the best grits," Richie informed the chief. "He uses milk and butter. You should have some."

"I already ate, thanks," Cutter said pleasantly. He would just as soon grits be declared illegal, but he was clearly in the minority in this household.

"Mom," the boy said, between spoonfuls, "are you staying for my birthday?"

That seemed to have blind-sided the woman. "Uh, sweetheart, that's two weeks from now. I, uh..."

"If she doesn't stay over that long," Ryan cut in, "we'll make sure to go down to Atlanta and see her."

"Or maybe," she said, patting her son's hand, as he sat near her, "I'll drive back here."

Richie's expression was hopeful. "But you might still *be* here."

Cutter certainly hoped he and his men wouldn't be.

"I might," Helen said lightly. "Now, eat your grits and drink your milk. It's a brand-new day, and you need a good start."

Richie drank some milk and then, grinning under a milk mustache, said to the chief, "I don't have to go to school today."

"That's nice," Cutter said, not knowing what else to say as the mother wiped the boy's face. "What will you do today, Richie?"

"Oh, I'm in training."

"Training...for what?"

"The Olympics."

"Special Olympics," Ryan said softly to Cutter. "I've fixed up a little work-out area in the attic for him. He's getting very fit."

Cutter grinned and said, "Well, that's great, Richie."

Cutter's man Jackson came in, frowning. "Chief?"

"Yes, Sergeant?"

The big cop jerked a thumb over his shoulder. "There's a UPS truck outside the gate, wanting to make a delivery. Needs to be signed for."

Cutter looked to Ryan. "You expecting a delivery?"

Ryan shrugged. "We get medical supplies regularly. It's nothing unusual."

Drawing closer to the table, Jackson said, "I don't think this is medical supplies. I eyeballed the package. It's pretty good size, crated up. I had a look at it and so did Buster. You know, considering the situation here."

"Buster?" Helen asked.

Cutter said, "Our Doberman Pinscher—our one-dog K-9 squad. Buster can sniff out nitro and plastic explosives and marijuana, too."

This time Helen raised only a single eyebrow. "A ten-man department with a bomb- and dope-sniffing dog?"

The chief chuckled. "One of our guys came back from Vietnam with him and we adopted them both. But I told you last night, Helen—we're a small but elite unit." Cutter got to his feet and faced Jackson. "Where's it from, Sergeant?"

"Return address is Chiapas, Mexico. From a Peter Potter."

"Uncle Pete!" the boy blurted.

"Oh, for Pete's sake," Helen said, smirking, shaking her head.

"Don't be redundant, honey," Ryan said. To Cutter

and Jackson, he said, "Pete Potter is my sister's husband. He's an archeologist and so is she. They've been in Mexico all year."

Richie had forgotten his half-eaten grits. "It's my *birthday* present! I bet it's my *birthday* present!"

Patiently, Helen explained to Cutter. "His uncle always sends Richard some oddball artifact from whatever dig he's on. For his birthday. Isn't that right, honey?"

Richie bobbed his head. "I have a whole collection in my room. I have a spear point..."

"From St. George Bay, Nova Scotia," his father said.

"...and a harpoon handle..."

"From Quinhagak, Alaska."

"...and a scary mask..."

"From the Judean Hills, Israel."

"...and a bunch of arrowheads!"

"South Carolina."

Richie was on his feet. "Do you wanna see, Chief Cutter? After I get my *new* gift, I mean." To his father, the boy asked, "Do I have to wait till my birthday to open it?"

His father frowned. "Well..."

Cutter said, "I think we probably *should* have a look inside that crate now."

"Why the hell not," Ryan said with a shrug.

"Dad," the boy said, "language."

His mother smiled.

Soon, in the living room, in the open space between the couch and the stairs, two officers lugged in a wooden crate stamped FRAGILE and THIS END UP and bearing the markings of passage between various ports and countries. It looked weathered, as if it had come from a war zone.

Following the two-man parade, another officer led Buster in. The Doberman waited and watched patiently for its own closer look at the contents. The dog was a friendly pooch and allowed the boy to pet it and in return slathered his face with a few long-tongue licks that made the child giggle.

Jackson handed Richie a sealed letter. "You're supposed to read this first, son."

The boy looked at his father, who was at his side. His dad nodded and Richie accepted the envelope from the officer, opened it carefully and withdrew a card.

In red letters against a light blue background, the card said *Feliz Cumpleaños* in a dialogue balloon pointing to a sombrero-sporting dog that was definitely not a Dober-man, rather a Chihuahua between two cacti.

The message inside the card was in cursive, which the boy could not read. He passed the card to his father, who took over.

"'Happy birthday, Mexico-style, to my favorite nephew from his favorite uncle. Here is your own genuine Aztec mummy. Treat him like a friend and he'll protect you. Love, Uncle Pete. P.S. This is a genuine arti-fact so don't let your mom put him out for the trash.'"

Helen just stood there with her arms folded, shaking her head, clearly annoyed but saying nothing. Mean-while, Ryan got a couple of claw hammers from some-where and the officers pried open the crate.

As the lid came slowly off, Richie leaned in anxious while his father restrained him gently and the dog sniffed the air and growled softly, more fear in the sound than menace.

Within the boxy crate, roped in place, seated in the bottom with his knees up, was a desiccated, mummified body with wisps of white hair, sunken eye sockets, a lack of lips exposing teeth in a terrible smile. The seated passenger in the box wore a moldering, once-colorful Aztec tunic over a withered once-white woven tunic.

"*Cool!*" the boy yelled as his mother simultaneously gasped in horror.

Cutter goggled at it, saying, "What in the hell is *this?*"

Hands on hips, wryly amused, Ryan was appraising the grisly contents of his brother's surprise package. "That's what we call in the medical trade a dead man, Chief. I'd say two- or three-hundred-years dead. But you can get the Medical Examiner out here if you'd like a second opinion."

Cutter gestured to the thing. "*This* is what your brother considers an appropriate gift for an impressionable kid?"

Ryan grunted a laugh. "Apparently. Pete's always been an individualist."

"A screwball is more like it."

Ryan shrugged. "One in every family, they say."

Helen was trembling and pointing to it she'd seen a ghost, and she wasn't near wrong. "Get that goddamn thing *out* of here!"

"Language," her husband said.

She spoke through her teeth, looking daggers at him. "It's a corpse. I won't have it in, in..."

"Your house?" Ryan with mild but unmistakable sarcasm. "*Not* your house, remember. Anyway, you were married to a medical student in another life. You've seen cadavers before."

Her disgust almost twisted the prettiness off her face. "Not any dead Aztec corpses I haven't. Get that thing *out* of here!"

"Doctor," Cutter said, stepping forward, "what are you going to do with this...this *whatever*-it-is."

"Dad," Richie said, still at his father's side, tugging at his father's sleeve. "Why is he sitting? Mummies are always standing on TV. When they aren't walking around slow and stuff."

"I'm no expert, Richie," Ryan said, "but I think Aztec mummies aren't like the Egyptian ones you see on TV and in the movies. Typically they were put in a sitting position, particularly if they were buried with a king or a prince, who they were guarding. It was out of respect."

"Can I keep him?"

"Oh my God," his mother said.

Rolling his eyes, Cutter said, "Roy, this thing being shipped, much less in your possession, is almost certainly illegal."

Ryan shrugged. "File your complaints with my brother-in-law. I'll give you contact info. He's still in Mexico. Of course he may be in some remote location. In any case, you could check with the authorities there."

Cutter managed a smile. "Come on now, Roy—don't be ridiculous..."

The doctor gestured at the open crate and its grisly contents. "Hey—I didn't ask for this thing. And that crate wasn't addressed to me, either. It's an unsolicited gift to my son. Of course, if you want an autopsy, I can perform it for you. No charge."

Sighing, Cutter raised his palms. "Ease off, Doc. It's just...you have some oddball relatives, it would seem."

Ryan's eyebrows went up. "That's just the husband. You should meet my sister."

That, anyway, got a nod out of Helen.

"Well," Cutter demanded of Ryan, "what do you think your goofy brother-in-law expected you to *do* with this thing? Make a conversation piece out of it? A clothes rack, maybe? Or let your boy add it to his collection in his room next to the harpoon handle?"

Seizing upon that last suggestion, the boy hugged his father's arm. "*Can* I keep him, Dad?"

"Son—please. Your mom is right to object to this 'gift' even being in the house. It's a dead person, after all."

Richie frowned up at his dad. "Not *new* dead. You said he died a long time ago, and Uncle Pete called him a mummy. Like on *Scooby-Doo!*"

Ryan lowered himself to a knee and looked right at his boy. "Son, this isn't a cartoon. It's very real. And this really *is* a dead person, however long ago he may have died."

Richie's brow tensed. "You mean maybe he *isn't* dead?"

"No, I mean...we can't be sure how very long ago it was that he died. Your uncle may know, and when he visits we can ask him. For now we should—"

"Get it," Helen said, arms folded again, standing well away from their seated intruder in his crate, "*out* of here."

Richie frowned at her, his chin crinkling in prelude to a cry. "Why don't you like him, Mom? He's friendly."

Her eyes widened. "Friendly?"

"Sure he is. Look at him! He's smiling!"

Ryan put an arm around his son's shoulder. "Richie, that's not a smile. It's just something that time and temperature have distorted into what kind of looks like a smile."

Cutter, realizing this was turning into a family matter better suited to a counselor than a cop, said, "Look, Roy — you need to decide what you're going to do with that thing. There isn't a museum in Atlanta that's appropriate for it. Maybe in New York or D.C., but—"

"I don't care *what* you do with it," Helen said, "just get it the hell out of here."

Richie started to say "Language" and his dad cautioned him not to with a gesture.

Then Ryan got to his feet and looked at Cutter. "Blake, this is an item of both historic and scientific interest. I'll look into where it belongs, and who might want it...when things settle down around here. Acceptable?"

Cutter let air out and nodded. "Acceptable."

Helen said, "Well, putting it in our son's *bedroom* is *not* acceptable."

"Perhaps," Ryan said to Cutter, "your men could haul our friend here up into the attic till I can research where to put him more permanently."

Cutter was already nodding. "Certainly. I'll organize that."

The boy was looking from the mummy to his mommy and his daddy and stopping there. "Can I play with him while he's here?"

Ryan shook his head firmly. "*No.* You have your stethoscope to fool around with, and your comic books to read, and there'll be homework delivered from school before long. You have plenty to do."

"But no friends to play with. They're all at school. And, anyway, I don't have that many friends."

"Maybe so. But at least the ones you *do* have are breathing."

Ryan was showing the officers bearing the crate and its contents up the winding stairs as Cutter went over to gather his Stetson and windbreaker. Helen followed him.

"Do me a favor, Chief? Blake?"

"Certainly, if I can."

"Look into what law my husband is breaking, allowing that...that *corpse* in the house."

"All right."

"And I may need your testimony."

Cutter frowned. "To what effect?"

"To my husband's negligence in allowing that thing to be kept under the same roof as our son."

He just nodded perfunctorily and went out, thinking, *And here I thought they were starting to get along....*

CHAPTER 5

The work-out equipment in the attic was gleaming and new in the dreary bare-wood space with its slanted roof and open beams. There was a stationary bike, a treadmill, a rowing machine, and a barbell set with a weight bench. Also a jump rope, curled on the floor like a snake. Richie thought the jump rope was for girls till his dad told him that wasn't so and showed him how to use it.

Richie's dad was planning to make a real room out of the attic—a do-it-yourself project that hadn't got done yet. For now, lots of boxes and trunks and stuff were piled at the far end, with the light of the single hanging bulb over where Richie did his exercises not reaching that far.

That end of the attic was spooky and Richie stayed away. His dad said the flooring back there wasn't so good, and that was another reason to stay at the other end with the gym stuff. So was the chugging air conditioner in the window. Before Dad put that in, it wasn't nice up here at all. Stuffy and musty and really, really hot.

But Dad had used soap and water and a bucket and

got the cobwebs out and used a hammer and nails and lumber to replace some floorboards. He hammered some nails back, too, that were sticking out and nasty.

Richie felt comfortable up here, at the gym end anyway, and was happy that the two policemen were hauling his birthday present up. At first he followed them from downstairs, then at the top showed them the way. Otherwise the policemen wouldn't have known where the door to the attic was. The door was in his room and that made it convenient for Richie with his mini-gym (as Dad called it) up there.

One of the policeman was tall and young and the other old and kind of pudgy. The old pudgy one made a lot of noise but the young one didn't as they carried the wooden box. Richie went on ahead up the narrow steep stairs to the attic and behind him there was some swearing from the pudgy old policeman. The young skinny one was in front coming up, carrying the box behind him, and kind of smiled at Richie when the old pudgy one said bad words.

Richie liked that. Not the bad words, but the young one smiling at him like there was a secret between them. Like he understood how older people could be.

They set the wooden box down where Richie's mini-gym ended and the storage area began. The pudgy one was huffing and puffing, but he got some words out.

"So now...now we're damn...damn *morticians*," he said. His hands were on his waist above his gun belt. "Wait till...till the police *union*...hears about...about *this*."

The pudgy policeman was sweating. The skinny one wasn't. It was pretty cool up there, the air conditioner on high.

The young one asked, "You don't really think that thing is for real, do you?" He wasn't breathing hard at all.

"You heard 'em talkin' down there. You heard the doc

and all that talk about his brother digging up shit in Mexico."

"Language," Richie said.

The pudgy policeman just looked at him. "Is this where you want it, kid?"

"Can you take him out?"

"Take who where?"

Richie pointed. "My friend. Lift him out and set him there. In front of those boxes?"

The pudgy policeman let out a whole bunch of air. The skinny one laughed. Not loud. Just one "ha."

"What if he comes apart," the pudgy policeman asked the skinny policeman, "in our hands?"

"Then he comes apart in our hands," the skinny policeman said and shrugged. "But we can't leave him in this crate."

"Why not?"

"Just do it, Lou. Be careful with that thing. It's even older than you are, y'know."

"Very funny."

The skinny one came around on the pudgy one's end and together they lifted the sitting mummy from the crate. Dust puffed off the figure like smoke. Both policemen made faces and turned their heads away. Richie's friend was in a kind of dress, Richie noted, very worn-out looking. No, more like kind of rotted but not rotted everywhere. The fancy color collar was faded but it was still cool. Even though that looked like a dress, Richie assumed this was a man. The white hair on top of his head was real short.

The skinny policeman pushed the mummy toward the pudgy one and said, "Kiss him, Lou."

The pudgy one made a face and turned away. "You *crazy* or something, Freddie?"

"Ah, he's only a dummy, you dummy."

Richie said, "Be careful with my friend." But at least now he knew his friend wasn't a girl. The skinny policeman had called him "him."

They set the mummy down on the wooden plank flooring in that same sitting position, backside on the floor, knees bent and up, feet on the floor, too. Then they slid the empty crate back with the other boxes and stuff. An old rocking horse of Richie's was back there between an old trunk and a fake Christmas tree.

The pudgy policeman wasn't breathing hard now. He looked at Richie, over by his stationary bike.

"I remember," the pudgy policeman said to the skinny policeman, "when kids *went* somewhere on their bike. Not *nowhere*."

Richie felt like he could say something about that even though they weren't speaking to him. They were speaking *about* him, so he said, "I have a bike. We live on the outskirts."

"So what?" the pudgy policeman said.

"So it's dangerous out here for a boy on a bike. Trucks and cars picking up speed. But Dad takes me to the park, sometimes. And then I ride my bike."

"Yeah, swell, good for you, kid. Is this piece of crap okay here?" The pudgy policeman gestured to Richie's seated friend.

The skinny policeman said, "If the chief hears you talking to that kid like that, Lou, you're gonna lose your goddamn pension."

"Language," Richie said softly.

"Yeah, yeah," the skinny policeman said. "So is he all right here, kid?"

"Yes."

More proof his friend was a boy. Or a man. The skinny policeman called the mummy "he."

The policemen headed for the well of the stairs, but Richie called out to them.

"And he *is* real."

The two policeman looked at him.

"And he's my *friend*."

"Sure he is," the skinny policeman said. Not mean. Just agreeing. But the pudgy policeman was shaking his head and muttering.

More bad language.

When they were gone, Richie went over and sat in front of the mummy. Both were sitting on the floor, mummy with knees up, Richie cross-legged. The light wasn't good here, but it wasn't bad either. He could see his friend but his friend's face didn't seem so scary like it did under a lot of light. His friend's eye holes were dark and Richie really kind of liked that big smile.

Richie stared at his friend's face and, after a while, he thought he could see something glowing in those eye holes.

———

At Helen's insistence, Roy walked with her outside to have a look at the footprints. The two cops who'd lugged the crate upstairs had rejoined the other two officers patrolling. The mugginess still lingered and the sun was high and hot now. The strange footprints were still there and Helen knelt over them.

She asked, "Could this be some horrible prank?"

He crouched beside her. "I don't follow."

"Maybe somebody *faked* these things."

He gave her a look. "You accusing me again of some bizarre stunt to—"

"No! No."

She stood and so did he. "But couldn't those prints come from boots or shoes of some kind?"

"Oh, Helen..."

With a raised palm, she said, "Hear me out. Could this be some kind of fear campaign? The grotesque footprints, the flaming projectile....Do you have enemies? Someone who owes you money for medical services on treatment they consider botched? Some husband whose wife died because he thinks you were negligent?"

His eyebrows climbed. "Oh, well thank you. Glad you have such a high opinion of me. No, my patients seem perfectly content with the quality of their medical care. Anyway, I *saw* whatever it was, remember....You *sketched* the damn thing! Or do you think I'm lying, or imagining things, or...what?"

She shook her head, frowned but not angrily. "No, no. Nothing like that. We're past such accusations. Could it have been a child? Some poor thing from Richard's special education class?"

"Are you serious?"

Her forehead tensed. "Some twisted child with a grudge against him...?"

"Right. Some kid Richie's age who has special needs problems but somehow fabricated monster boots and put together a creature-feature get-up, fright wig and all. Just getting a jump on Halloween."

She sighed, shook her head again, laughed bitterly. "I know how I sound."

He slipped his arm around her. "Like a mother crazy with concern for her child. It'd be unnatural otherwise."

"Something unnatural *is* happening here. Roy, we have to protect Richard."

"Damn straight we do."

They walked to the front of the house, Roy's arm still around her.

She said, "I'm going to spend the afternoon with Richard. Drawing, doing crafts. He's probably up in the attic with that awful thing." She shivered. "I could just *kill* your brother-in-law. *And* your sister!"

It was Roy's turn to sigh. "He meant well. But, yeah— that was over the line even for Pete."

Her eyes lifted to the ceiling. "I want you to go up there and make sure that child is not...not *fooling* with that disgusting thing. Will you please?"

"I will, I will."

"And get it out of here tomorrow."

On the porch, they paused before going in.

"Can you busy yourself this afternoon?" she asked him.

He nodded, gesturing to the cement-block outbuilding where he maintained his practice. "I'm going to make some calls from my office. Let my nurse and receptionist know that they're on paid leave till this settles down. Call the other two family practice docs in town and make arrangements for my patients. Call a couple of specialists in Atlanta to take over certain key cases. I have plenty to do."

"All right." She sighed and her smile was small and sad. "Pity it took a bunch of dead doctors and a murder threat against our son to bring us together."

He studied her. "Are we? Together?"

"Where the welfare of our son is concerned? We may disagree about the 'how,' but not that there's a need. And responsibility."

They went inside and Roy headed upstairs and went to his son's room. The walls had posters of TV shows and movies Richie liked—*Star Trek*, *Batman* (the old Adam West one), *Scooby Doo*. The boy kept a neater room than most his age and was protective of his comic books, which were in neat piles atop a low-slung bookcase filled with Little Golden Books and Dr. Seuss.

But the child, predictably, was not there.

And the stethoscope, so precious and compelling to the boy the night before, lay abandoned on his bed. At least Richie had made his bed, which was one of his regular chores.

Roy went quietly up the stairs and heard his son's voice: "I'm going to do Track and Field at the Olympics. I do a lot of running in the yard to get ready. And Dad got me all this stuff to get in shape...."

Roy entered the attic, Richie hearing him immediately. The boy, who'd been sitting Indian-style in front of the ghostly-looking mummy—which looked like a refugee from the end of *Psycho*—sprang to his feet and turned to his dad. The child's smile indicated he knew he'd been caught doing something maybe he shouldn't.

"Hi, Dad. I was just talking to my friend. Do you know his name?"

Roy walked over to Richie. "No, son, I don't. Your uncle didn't put that in his birthday note to you. I'm guessing your gift's name is lost to time."

"Oh. Well, he doesn't need to have a name to be my friend, does he?"

"No, but you do understand he's a *pretend* friend, son. He's not alive."

"I thought you said—"

He put both hands on the boy's shoulders. "I told you before that you'd misunderstood me. He was once alive, of course, but we don't know exactly when he died. He's not a toy or a plaything."

"No. He's my friend."

"*Pretend* friend." He put his arm around his son's shoulder, putting the mummy to both their backs. "He was a real living breathing someone once, and it would be disrespectful to play games with him."

"I wasn't playing games."

"I know. But go on down to your room now. We'll be having lunch soon and then your mom wants to do some art and crafts with you. Spend the afternoon with her favorite son."

"I'm her *only* son."

"Right. But that doesn't mean you're not her favorite."

The boy was uncharacteristically sullen as he walked down the attic stairs, but at least he'd obeyed.

Roy tousled his son's hair as he passed through the bedroom on his way downstairs. He had a lot of work to do this afternoon in putting his practice on hold, and he was pleased his wife would be spending some quality time with their boy. Maybe she'd realize just how much she and her father underestimated Richie.

At least she might if the kid kept his mouth shut about that mummy being his pal and still alive....

———

They had spaghetti for supper, a favorite of Richie's and a specialty of his mother's, and the evening was quiet and homey—the only fire being the one in the fireplace. Helen reported her afternoon with their son in loving detail, Roy went quickly over what he'd accomplished with his work, and Richie watched TV in the book-lined study.

Helen went up to bed early, around nine o'clock, which was Richie's bedtime. They tucked the boy in together and Roy said goodnight to his wife at the guest room door. Then he went downstairs, fixed himself a highball, thought about how much he still loved that woman, fixed himself another highball, and after while went back upstairs.

He knocked at the guest room door.

She said, "Yes," and he went in. She was in a negligee with her covers at her waist, the full breasts discreetly covered by the garment but still a formidable presence in the room. Roy came over and, rather boldly, sat on the edge of the bed near her.

She nodded around the room, where three of her framed landscapes hung, including the Hawaiian one she'd painted on their honeymoon. "I'm a little surprised to see so much of my artwork on the walls. I kind of thought they'd be stowed away in the attic."

"Then where would I put my brother's gift?"

She actually chuckled at that. "What about my self-portrait?"

"It's in my bedroom. Care for a look?"

Her smile was crinkly. "Don't get ahead of yourself..."

He leaned in. "Okay. Look, I know this has already been an awful ordeal, but I was thinking—really, we're in a better place with this thing now, since that attack last night."

Her eyes grew big. "Really? That was a help was it, that flaming bottle of gasoline?"

He nodded. "It gives the police something tangible to deal with. Up till now they thought the doctors might be accidental deaths—now they're talking serial murder. It has their attention."

"And you have mine." She sat forward and those breasts came along for the ride. "But, Roy—nothing's changed. We're still legally separated and the reasons for that remain. We'll always be Richard's parents, but anything else is...well, we need to face it....It's over."

He shook his head slowly. "It sure doesn't feel like it. And even if that's so, we have a son in the middle. Right now he doesn't know what the hell's happening between us—never mind that he's the target of some mentally deranged loon who was able to murder three medical men."

"Roy..."

"I'm just saying...let's not make it any tougher on Richie than it already is. Let's just keep it friendly between us, even if it's only us playing a game. To keep the boy from getting tied up into knots."

She leaned back and crossed her arms over the shelf of her bosom. "If you're talking about maintaining appearances in front of our son, that's a game I can play. But if you think you're climbing into this bed tonight, buddy boy, you are on the losing end."

That hurt. He knew he probably deserved it, but it damn well hurt, and the two highballs fueled his response as he got to his feet: "Honey, you better get over yourself. Get something straight, if you can get out in front of that overblown ego of yours. Right now you're nothing to me but my son's mother, a biological reality I can't do anything about at this point. And I have about as much romantic interest in you as a potted plant."

Her frown was like a fist clenching. "I don't have to put up with this crap...."

"Then don't. But the last time you walked out on me, when things got a bit too tough for your sensitive nature? You wound up on the wrong side of a custody battle. And if you walk out now, honey, you might find out that whatever's out there in the dark wanting to take me and our kid down might just be waiting for you. He might've decided you make a pretty attractive alternative target."

Her chin was quivering and her eyes threatened to overflow. "That was a lousy goddamn thing to say...."

He shrugged grandly. "I'm just being realistic. So play *nice*...and I don't mean bedroom games."

He was at the door when she said, "Roy?"

He turned and looked at her. If he'd ever seen a

woman more beautiful, he couldn't remember when. "What?"

"...Don't go."

"Huh," he said. "Seems to me that's the same request I made of you six months ago."

And he left her there with her paintings and her memories and, just maybe, her tears.

In the attic, Richie in his pajamas was kneeling before his mummified friend. The boy had the stethoscope around his neck.

"Nobody around here likes you except me," the boy said. "But I don't care. And you shouldn't either. My name's Richie and I wish I knew your name. I could make one up, but I don't know any Aztec names. And everybody seems to have forgot yours, anyway."

Richie looked at the claw-like hands, the gaping mouth with its Halloween grin, the empty eye sockets that had seemed to glow before but were just black holes now.

"You don't look so good," the boy said. "I'm going to be a doctor someday. Like my dad. So maybe I better take a look at you."

He held the stethoscope's chest piece to bony ribs and listened.

And listened.

And listened.

Was that a heartbeat he heard?

Then he paused in his examination and said, "Y'know, pal—I think you're going to be all right."

———

In the trees near the walled-in yard and house, facing the side of the old house where the window air-conditioner chugged in an attic window, a Southern Magnolia ruled, a good eighty-feet tall with a spread of fifty feet, its evergreen leaves large, and lustrous even after dark, shimmering with moonlight.

Beautiful.

Up its trunk clambered something not beautiful, unseen on its ascent and all but invisible when it settled onto a branch providing a good view of the house, and the window through which he—because this watcher was not really an "it"—had on previous unrecorded visits seen through his binoculars the figure of the boy, moving from one exercise station to another.

Dennis—for that was the name of the man who some within that house described as a "creature"—had once done exercises himself. Had built muscles on a frame thought too fragile for such a thing. Had developed dexterity for himself through long hard work. He understood the boy and he could, in a way, identity with him.

Pity the child had to die.

CHAPTER 6

The Doberman, Buster, was tied up outside the wall to act as an overnight guard dog along the line of trees from which the strange footprints had led and returned. The chain had enough length to allow the animal to get right up to the edge of the wooded area, and at the moment the animal was sniffing around a certain Southern Magnolia.

The four officers on duty patrolling the Ryan grounds tonight were divided up in teams of two on either side of the fieldstone wall. They walked patrol separately and only occasionally checked in with each other. None of those four were near Buster at the moment, who had not barked to alert them and even now the animal's growling was low and rumbling. Mostly Buster was sniffing, as if looking for somewhere to lift a leg.

So no negligence on the part of the officers added to what happened next...

...when a black shape with long arms and clawed splayed fingers dropped down like a big blunt rock on the back of the dog, surprising it, eliciting only a single yipe before those clawed digits dug into the Doberman's throat, turning a

dangerous adversary into a quivering helpless mass and powerful hands gripped and twisted and choked and finally snapped bones as if they were nothing more than brittle sticks.

Out in front of the house, at the bottom of the steps up onto the porch, the two cops who earlier had carted the crate upstairs were comparing notes and grabbing smokes and complaining about their very long day, with less than half an hour before the next shift of four officers came on.

Skinny Fred frowned, looked up, saying, "What the hell was *that?*"

Pudgy Lou, exhaling Marlboro smoke, said, "What the hell was what?"

"Didn't you hear anything?"

Lou blew a Bronx cheer. "Birds and bugs and beasties in the woods, kiddo. What do you expect in the boonies?"

Fred was looking toward the wooded area, treetops visible over beyond the wall, a mass of leaves shimmering in night breeze, catching some moonlight and throwing it around.

"Guess you're right, Lou. Anything moves out there, Buster's sure to let us know."

Lou grunted affirmatively. "We got four guys on foot patrol, and Cutter added two cars to work the highway and the back roads within a few miles, either side. Nothing's getting past us, kiddo. Nothin'."

With a sigh, Fred pitched his smoke sparking into the night. "Yeah, but we're all gettin' punchy. That's a lot of long hours for everybody. We're back on at *eight* tomorrow morning."

"No rest for the wicked," Lou observed, grinning like he just thought that up.

———

The terrible hands drew away from the animal's throat. The human creature, though low to the ground, nonetheless hovered over the limp bag of fur and flesh and bones that had been a living breathing and dangerous creature moments before.

He faced the fieldstone wall and his head went back, his eyes lifting to the attic window.

A light was on.

That boy was up past his bedtime.

Bad boy. Bad boy.

The human creature patted the dead dog.

Good boy. Good boy.

———

In his pajamas, Roy—the buzz of the two highballs wearing off, embarrassed about how things had deteriorated in his guest-room conversation with Helen—thought he'd better check on his son before hitting the sack himself.

Yet not only were the boy's lights still on, and the bed still made, Richie wasn't there! But some light bled from under the door to the attic.

Shaking his head, Roy went up.

Richie was kneeling at the seated desiccated corpse, listening at its chest with the stethoscope. The thing in the faded Aztec collar and thin white tunic seemed to grin at Roy, as if to say, *You can't compete with me, you pitiful human daddy.*

"Son," Roy said.

Richie didn't hear him, the ear tips of the stethoscope in place.

"*Son!*"

The boy swung his head around, startled. "Uh. Oh. Hi, Dad."

"Yeah, hi. It's way after your bedtime, your know."

Richie shrugged, smiled. "I know. I kinda lost track."

Roy's fists were on his hips. "Well, you need to get *back* on track. What are you doing there, anyway?"

Richie bobbed his head toward the seated mummy. "Playing doctor."

Definitely not the way Roy had played doctor when he was a kid.

The father went to the boy and knelt, the mummy nearby, wearing its mocking expression.

"Listen," Roy said, "you can't be up here. Not at this hour. And you *know* how your mother feels about your...your friend here."

"I know, but *you* don't feel like that. Do you, Dad?"

He put some firmness into his voice. "I should have put a stop to this before. It's disrespectful." He gestured to the grinning corpse. "This was a human *being*, son. You don't 'play,' not 'doctor' or anything else, with an actual dead person."

Richie was shaking his head. "But, Dad, he's *not* dead, he's *alive*."

Roy frowned. "I told you, Richie. Your friend here died hundreds of years ago."

The boy winced in thought, obviously confused. "So is he *still* alive? Or is he alive *again*? Like Dracula or Jesus?"

Right now Roy could really use another highball.

But instead he just got to his feet, pointed toward the stairwell, and said, "Never mind any of that. *Out.* Oh-you-tee. No more talk! And *stay* out of this attic."

The boy appeared to be on the verge of tears. "What about the Olympics? I'm in *training!*"

The father closed his eyes, sighed, opened his eyes and said, "You can come up here when it's daytime...but stay down at the mini-gym end, okay?"

"Okay." Then Richie came back and spoke with a

heart-breaking earnestness: "But I'm trying to tell you about my *friend*."

"What about him?"

"That he's *alive!* Dad, you need to *listen*."

"I *am* listening."

"No!" The boy lifted the stethoscope around his neck by the chest piece. "You need to listen through *this*."

Roy shook his head. Pointed to the stairs. "Out!"

The boy frowned. "Boy! Some doctor *you* are...."

———

Officer Fred Dickson, making his final sweep of the night of the exterior wall, got to thinking—that yipe had sounded canine. Not some bird or bug or "beastie," either....

Maybe, the slender cop thought, *I better check on Buster*....

Flashlight in hand, he went to where the metal stake held the animal's chain in place, finding no sign of the dog. And Buster wasn't over at his water and kibble dishes by the wall, either.

Yet the chain stretched toward the trees, pulled fairly taut.

Working his flash's beam on the ground, Fred followed that chain as if it were a pointing finger. And that pointing finger led to the Doberman, sprawled on its side at the edge of the woods under the overhanging leafy branches of the big Magnolia tree. The dog's eyes were open but unseeing, its tongue draped out of its mouth like a slice of rare meat.

The officer crouched by the beast, inspected it, found it dead all right, not just sick or drugged, but with its neck at an impossible angle—*good Lord, could* hands *have broken that sinewy neck?* —and then rose and stared into the timber. Seeing nothing, he craned his neck and sent the beam up the trunk and into the leaf-thick branches and a dark shape came down on him, like a one-boulder avalanche.

The flashlight flew from Fred's fingers as he hit the ground hard, where he tried to get the thing off him, off his back, trying to squirm out from under, and when that didn't work, he bucked and bucked and finally the thing rolled off. Then huge hard savage fists were pummeling his knees and thighs, and he swung fists down into what appeared to be a torso and bushy-haired head and not much else, getting grotesque glimpses of his opponent as the bizarre fistfight traveled in and out of the fallen flashlight's beam.

And in one horrible moment Officer Dickson got a good look at the half-man's face and it froze him just long enough for his fierce, stubby opponent to go scrambling off into the darkness of the wooded area.

Lou Rawley came running up, the pudgy cop breathing hard by the time he got to his partner, who'd fallen to his knees.

"Fred! What in hell *happened?*"

His partner was panting. "That...that *thing* came right down out of that damn tree and landed on me!"

"*What* thing?"

The officer shivered. "I don't know...I really don't know....Just...it was some kind of a...hell, I don't know *what* it was!"

The pudgy officer helped the skinny officer to his feet and asked him, "Are you okay? You need me to rustle up the doc? Or get you to an emergency room...?"

"I'm...I'm fine. Well, not fine, but...just bruises and some nicks and, Lou, I am *freaking* out!"

Lou slipped a supportive arm around his partner's

shoulder. "Take it easy, boy. Now. Describe what attacked you."

"It was big. And small...."

Lou made a face. "What?"

"Look, I just caught *glimpses* of it. I dropped my flashlight, right at the start, and mostly we fought in the dark. But he was no bigger than this."

Fred held a hand up to his mid-thigh.

Then the young cop went on: "Came down on me from that tree. Dropped right on me!"

Lou grinned, but an uneasy grin. "Musta scared the living hell out of you—that's natural, even as lightweight a little guy as he must've been."

"Oh, but he *wasn't* light—he was heavy as a ton of bricks, man. Shoulders out to here! He *flattened* me. Whatever it is, it's a strong son of a bitch. Take a look at Buster and see."

Lou did that.

The older cop came back with all the blood drained out of his face. "It *must* be strong if it could do that to a Doberman."

"He *has* to be."

"'He?' You said 'it' before."

"That was no animal. No monkey or ape, either. That was some kind of person."

———

Somehow Chief Blake Cutter wasn't even surprised finding himself in the middle of the night seated on the couch at the Ryan place with Helen Ryan perched between him and her husband. The woman was in a pink dressing gown and, even at this hour, woken from bed, with no make-up on at all, her hair a blonde tangle, she was strikingly beautiful. That doctor ought to get his act together and woo this doll back.

But that wasn't any of Blake Cutter's business—the murderous attacker terrorizing this place was.

Helen had a nine-by-twelve-inch sketch book in her lap and a charcoal pencil in her right hand, acting as police artist while the still somewhat shell-shocked Officer Dickson described what he'd seen.

The lanky young officer had already received a post-attack check-up from the doctor, who found nothing but some contusions and a few scrapes—nothing, anyway, that some soap, water, Bacitracin, and a few bandages couldn't handle.

Helen turned her sketch in the pad around toward the young cop, who sat nearby in a straight-back chair. What she'd drawn was an excellent depiction of something terrible—a figure with long stringy yet bushy black hair, a round, grooved, flat-nosed, scruffy bearded face with dark eyes under a shelf of forehead where big shaggy black eyebrows dwelled. Wide mouth, irregular teeth. Broad shoulders and a well-developed torso all in black —a sweater possibly, large bare feet, toes spread out, hands the same, splayed and sharp-nailed.

Helen asked the officer, "Is that about right?"

"Yes...I only saw flashes of it, but...yes."

"No sense of legs?"

"No. Feet, but no legs."

Cutter leaned out and, speaking across Mrs. Ryan, asked Dr. Ryan, "Does that tally with what you saw, Doc?"

A fire was going in the fireplace and all of them were serving as screens for the reflections of flames making abstract art of them.

Ryan nodded slowly but repeatedly. "The officer here

got a better look than I did, but...yes. What Helen has drawn is an accurate representation of what I saw."

"What about this lack of legs? Feet and no legs? How is that possible?"

The doctor flipped a hand. "If it's an amputee, perhaps prosthetics, unusually small, compact...hidden by the tugged-down garment. If a dwarf, stubby legs that the sweater might hide or simply be unseen, the individual being so close to the ground. We're talking low lighting, the officer under assault from a low-lying attacker."

The chief leaned back. "All right, then. You're a doctor. If you were to see something, *someone*, like this—a patient maybe...what would you call it?"

"I'd call it 'him.'"

Cutter raised a palm in mild surrender. "All right. Him. We're not dealing with a creature or a beast, but I never thought we were. This is a human being. Do you know of cases of deformed human beings like this?"

The doctor's shrug seemed almost in slow motion. "I know *of* them. And we're only guessing about what precisely these birth defects might be."

Cutter thought about that. "Might someone burdened by severe birth defects blame those defects on the doctor who delivered him?"

Ryan nodded. "It's possible. And the parents, of course."

"Or maybe...doctors in general?"

"Perhaps." Ryan thought a moment or two. "Or more likely—as Helen theorized earlier—specifically specialists in pediatrics. And you're looking for links between the three murdered medics, aren't you, Blake?"

Cutter nodded, once. "We are. But if you feel we've established that the assailant who struck here is in fact a deformed individual, that narrows the search." He took the sketch book from Helen and held up the nightmare image. "It shouldn't be too difficult to locate someone who answers to *this* description, should it?"

"No," Roy said. "They'd require special training, specific therapy...but there could be a hitch."

"Like how?"

The doctor let in and out slowly. "It's not as bad as it once was, but in the old days, particularly? A family might never let it be known that one of theirs bore the 'sin' or 'embarrassment' of congenital deformities such as these. Cruel, backward thinking might lead to hiding a child away—think of the gothic horror stories where some poor twisted member of the family was sequestered away in an attic or institution."

A quick look passed between husband and wife.

Then the doctor went on: "A child raised under such restrictive, hurtful conditions could itself become twisted. If you tell someone they're ugly long enough, they may *become* ugly...inside."

No one said anything for a while.

Finally, Cutter said, "Thank you, doctor, for your insights. And thank you, Mrs. Ryan, for sharing your artistry. We're quite fortunate to have an artist as talented as you right at hand. We'll get this sketch circulated to all medical facilities statewide."

The young cop asked, "Chief—what about distributing that to the media?"

Cutter frowned. "You want to start a panic, Dickson? And if the national media gets a whiff, there'll be a fleet of TV trucks down here and we'll be crawling with reporters. 'Halloween Comes Early to Southern Hamlet!' Not a word, get me?"

"I got you, Chief."

From behind the couch, Richie suddenly leaned over,

a wide-eyed child in *Six Million Dollar Man* pajamas. "Boy, does *that* guy look weird!"

Helen turned the sketchbook face down on her lap. "Roy, get your son out of here! I don't want him *seeing* this."

Of course he already had, Cutter thought.

But Richie was leaning across the back of the couch even more. "If that's a bad guy you're after, Chief Cutter, and you put him in a cage or something?" He looked at his mom eagerly. "Can I have that drawing for my room? I'll put him up by the *Incredible Hulk!*"

She ignored that, though the boy's sideways face was next to her. She turned away, toward her husband, and said, "Roy, deal with this. It's bad enough Richard saw that *other* horrible thing upstairs!"

"Ah, Mom. He's my friend. He's not hurting anything. He's just sitting around."

Now she swung round to face the boy. "You get back to bed. Right now!"

The child's expression grew pouty. "You guys were making a lot of noise down here. You woke me up. It wasn't *my* fault."

"I don't care whose fault it was," she said, "you get back to bed."

Richie repositioned himself on the other side of his mother to address his father. "Dad, don't I have any rights?"

"You have the right to remain silent," he said, "and go to bed. Or maybe get a swat of my right hand across your tail."

The boy raised his hands in surrender. "I understand those rights."

And he went slowly up the stairs.

"Where'd he get *that?*" Helen asked her husband.

"TV," he said. He turned to Chief Cutter. "This makes

two attacks in two days. What do you suggest we do now?"

"You double-check all windows and doors," Cutter said. "Both floors. I'll get a support team from the Atlanta suburbs and cover a wider swath, including that wooded area our intruder came out of both nights."

Helen asked, "Is there any chance that it...*he's*...gone now?"

Roy picked up on that. "Our visitor knows we've increased security and that he'll really be up against it here on out. Maybe that'll be enough to scare him away."

Cutter looked from the husband's face to the wife's and back again. "Doctor...Helen...whatever it is we're after has killed before. We know that now. We also know we have a shrewd adversary whose motives are irrational and yet focused. I'm afraid it will take a bullet...probably more than 'a' bullet...to stop him. He has specific targets and the next two on his list are you, Roy, and...I'm sorry...but your son."

Ryan was frowning deep. "What are our odds in this, Chief? As you see it?" He glanced at his wife. "We have a right to know."

Cutter got to his feet. "In our favor...as long as we can keep you isolated, and covered."

And everybody went off to catch a few hours of sleep.

Or at least try to.

CHAPTER 7

Roy still had work to do in his one-doctor clinic in the cement-block building to one side of the big old house. He'd determined to call each of his patients personally and assure them the physicians he was referring them to would be more than up to the task of filling in for him, and that he should be available again for consultation before too very long. The vagueness of this was obviously not terribly reassuring, but virtually all of his patients appreciated him making the effort.

Of course he'd been vague as well about the reason for the indefinite hiatus in his practice, saying simply, "I have some family matters to deal with." Most all of his patients—probably most of the population of Peachtree Heights—knew that those "family matters" likely had to do with his wealthy estranged wife and their special boy. But no one was tactless enough to bring any of that up.

Word about the attacks at the Ryan compound didn't seem to have gotten out, which in such a small town was a big miracle. But Chief Cutter ran a tight ship and his men, many of them NYPD early retirees Cutter had worked with during his tenure on that department, knew how and when to keep the lid on.

Roy and his wife, since the guest room blow-up last night, had kept out of each other's way ever since. Oh, they'd shared a quiet, polite breakfast in the company of their chipper son—the husband making breakfast again, eggs and bacon and toast this time—and Helen had found a quiet corner in the big living room to do sketches for a painting she was planning. Richie said he was going to read comic books and then do his Special Olympics training.

"Please stay away," his mother said to her son, "from that thing up there."

Richie started to answer but his father gave him a look that said it was best not to get into this with his mother. His son took the hint. And of course Roy knew, for all his blustering at the boy, that Richie would no doubt spend a good deal of time talking to his "friend."

As long as his friend doesn't enter the conversation, Roy thought wryly, *we're probably okay....*

Lovely in a pink pants suit, her hair pony-tailed back, Helen fixed lunch—tomato soup and grilled cheese sandwiches. The conversation ran to Richie again saying he wanted to go to the park and go rowing when "Dad gets over the flu." The child also commented on how nice it was of his mother to come and be his daddy's nurse.

She'd let that pass with an "Um-hmmm."

Chief Cutter showed up after lunch and, as Helen worked with Richie with the homework assignments that had been delivered and on his coloring books in the study-cum-library area of the living room, the officer and the doctor took the couch by the unlighted fire for an update. Roy was in a white polo and off-white slacks that unintentionally gave him a medical look; Cutter, his usual shirt-and-tie and chinos.

"I've enlisted some help," Cutter said, still in his windbreaker but with the Stetson in his lap, "from several Atlanta suburbs."

"Not the Atlanta PD itself?"

Cutter made a slight face. "I can do that you insist, Roy, but I frankly prefer to keep in charge of this thing myself, and bolstering my team with these suburban troops allows me to work closely with you. The Atlanta boys would likely blow in and roll over both of us."

Nodding, Roy said, "I'm content with what you're doing, Blake. How are you deploying these extra men?"

"Some'll be here on the grounds. Detective Janet Hodges from Buford is following up by phone on some leads and a detective from Decatur is going over the files of the three deceased doctors, looking for tie-ups. But I also have a roadblock set up, checking anyone who approaches the road past your house, and then shooting them off on a detour."

"Well, that's fine, but you don't *really* expect our sawed-off intruder to drive a car, do you?"

Cutter shrugged. "Vehicles can be customized for little people—pedal extenders, hand controls, thick seat cushions to enable seeing over the steering wheel."

"Yes, I'm aware of that," Roy said, just a little insulted, "but we have a pretty specific idea of what this individual looks like. You've circulated my wife's sketch?"

"Of course," Cutter said, no happier at being underestimated than Roy had been.

"Well, would our half-man risk being stopped at a roadblock? Or being spotted?"

Cutter cocked his head. "Let's say this is a little person with a grudge against doctors, specific doctors like yourself, as we've theorized. For one thing, he's wearing black and striking at night. And he may be making his appearance seem more fearsome on purpose, to better terrorize your household."

"I hadn't considered that seriously," Roy admitted.

Cutter nodded over toward the library where Richie was on the floor hunkered over an *Emergency!* coloring book. "Is your son at all aware of what's been going on?"

"No. He's all caught up with his new 'friend,' the Aztec mummy." Roy shook his head, sighed a laugh. "I've been trying to get him to keep away from the grisly thing, and Helen wants it out of here, like *now*."

Cutter frowned thoughtfully. "It's none of my business, but...no. It's none of my business."

"Of course it's your business, Blake. What?"

The chief took air in, let it out. "Maybe postpone getting rid of it. Maybe it's not entirely a bad thing, having something to distract the boy. Till we get a handle on this thing. Till we catch this bastard."

Roy hadn't considered that, either.

But now he did.

"Okay," he said reluctantly. "I'll lay off a little. But it's not healthy. Hell, it's not sanitary."

Cutter was just getting up to leave when a knock came at the front door. The chief, Stetson still in hand, waited by the couch while the doctor answered the knock.

Sgt. Leon Jackson, Cutter's man-in-charge at the scene, nodded to Roy, who gestured for him to step inside.

"Dr. Ryan," the uniformed officer said, "I need a word with the chief, if you don't mind."

"Certainly."

Roy traded places with Cutter, who then huddled near the front door talking sotto voce with his second-in-command. Then the chief came over and rejoined his host.

"Doc, your father-in-law's at the gate wanting to be let in. We've checked his ID and he's who he says he is." Cutter half-grinned. "And he's driving a Lincoln Continental, which supports his claim even better than his driver's license."

"What good are roadblocks," Roy muttered, "if you're going to let just *anybody* through."

The chief gave up half a grin and said, "I'll admit him, with your permission."

"Please do." Although it sounded more like "Please kill me."

Cutter raised an eyebrow. "You want me to stick around? Back you up? Answer any questions he may have?"

"No. Thank you, but I'll handle this."

The chief tugged on his hat, slipped outside, went down the steps and got into his gray Dodge Challenger. Moments later, he was pausing at the gate to allow the new visitor passage.

The silver Lincoln, with Alexander Parsons himself at the wheel—the man was rich enough to have a chauffeur, but Atlanta just wasn't that kind of town—rolled in and settled on the gravel apron near the porch, where Roy stood waiting, arms folded.

Parsons climbed out into a perfect, sunny day that didn't seem to impress him, a big, handsome man in his early sixties in Ray-Bans, his silver-gray hair swept back, his wide-lapel suit light gray with blue pinstripes, his tie a matching blue, his shirt white with blue stripes. He looked like a million bucks, but was worth plenty more.

At the foot of the porch steps, the CEO of one of Atlanta's biggest businesses glanced up and said, "Roy," and nodded, as if acknowledging a door man.

"Alex," the doctor said, returning the nod, as his father-in-law strode up the groaning steps, grimacing just a little, as if the shape the old house was in indicated what a failure his daughter had married.

Neither man initiated the handshake ritual—the nods would suffice.

"May I come in?" Parsons asked, making it barely a question. "I'd like to speak to you and my daughter."

Not *with—to.*

"Certainly," his son-in-law said.

Now Roy really did serve as literal doorman.

Helen, sitting in the library on the floor with her similarly seated son, looked over, saw her father coming in with her husband trailing, and her eyes popped. She got to her feet. Richie didn't notice.

"Dad," she breathed, barely audible from the distance between the front door and library portion of the vast living room.

Richie turned away from his coloring book and saw who had arrived. He got to his feet slowly and winced as he considered what his grandfather showing up here, in enemy territory, might mean.

But then human emotion took over and the boy ran to his grandfather and gave him a hug around the waist. Alexander Parsons smiled, faintly, tousled the boy's hair.

This is where, Roy thought, moving away from them, *a human being would crouch and meet the boy at eye level.*

Instead, Parsons just looked down at his grandson—who looked up at him like a young mirror—and said, "Have you been a good boy?"

"Pretty good, Grandpa. Pretty good."

"Very nice to see you." Then Parsons seemed uncomfortable, possibly realizing he hadn't brought a gift of any sort for the boy. The grandfather dug in his pocket and came back with a five-dollar bill. "Here's something for you, Richard."

"Thanks, Grandpa." Richie looked at it, his eyes

bright with the possibility of the comic books he could buy.

Parson raised a finger and again smiled faintly. "Don't spend it all in one place."

"I won't, Grandpa."

He gestured vaguely toward the library. "Now, run off and go back to doing what you were doing. I need a little time with your mother and father. For some grown-up talk."

"Yes, Grandpa."

And Richie ran back to resume his coloring in the library, where his mother was still standing as frozen as Lot's wife.

Her father summoned his daughter with a curling finger and walked toward the couch, passing his son-in-law like a vehicle in the slow lane and saying, "Come along, Roy."

Parsons settled on the couch, patted the cushion next to him and, with a look, informed his daughter that she should sit there, which she did. Roy pulled up a chair, positioning himself between them, the unlit fireplace to his back.

"Does the boy know," Parsons said, quietly, "about these attacks?"

"No," Roy said. "But you do, apparently."

"Belatedly," Parsons said, eyes narrowing. "I had to hear about it from my sources, and then not till this morning."

That had been after Cutter brought other cops in from the suburbs—the chief couldn't keep as tight a lid on with the outsiders in the mix.

Helen told her father, "We didn't want to concern you."

"Very thoughtful," her father said, dryly. He looked pointedly at Roy. "Well, this stops *now*....I'm going to take my grandson and his mother with me, back to Atlanta, to our home, where I can provide professional security of a standard appropriate to a horrific situation like this. And with the full support of the Atlanta police."

"Richie is staying here," Roy said. He had long since stopped allowing Alexander Parsons to roll over him. "And Helen is welcome to stay."

"How generous of you," Parsons said.

Helen looked from one man to another as each spoke, as if she were watching a tennis match she'd bet heavily on.

Roy shrugged. "The boy likes having his mom around. As unfortunate as these circumstances are, mother and son are spending time together and that's a positive."

Parsons shook his head, not in disagreement just general disgust, his upper lip curling back bitterly. "You would put the safety of my grandson and daughter in the hands of a bunch of bump-in-the-road hick police? You've been irresponsible in the past, Roy, but now you've really outdone yourself."

Roy didn't flinch. "Chief Cutter has taken personal charge. He's former NYPD and so is much of his staff. He's filling in with other neighboring departments and I'm satisfied he, and they, are up to the job."

The older man huffed a disparaging laugh. "That's a blatantly ludicrous assessment. My understanding is that you've had a note threatening my grandson, and a bomb thrown through a window..."

"A Molotov cocktail, yes, which I promptly threw back out."

"...with a police dog strangled last night, and an officer badly beaten. And an apparent tie to the three previous murders of those doctors. You're under siege here! And this, this...*creature* is still out there."

"He is." Roy shifted in his chair. "But every effort is being made—"

"What if," Parsons said, his tone suddenly reasonable, "I remove Richard from the sphere of this threat? To somewhere out of state? Some secure, secret location where he could be properly guarded and protected?"

Roy waved that off. "He's guarded and protected here. Anyway, taking Richie out of this environment might confuse and badly disorient him. You have no idea how he has grown and flourished in these last six months."

The upper lip curled back again. "Away from *my* influence, you mean."

"You said that, not me. But he's going to school with other children now, not being sequestered and tutored and psychologically poked and prodded. He's becoming a normal little boy."

Parsons grunted a non-laugh. "Going to school with other 'special needs' students. What in God's name is normal about that? Roy, you've never been able to face reality. Richard took forever to walk, to talk, he lagged way behind in so many areas..."

"He's made strides. He is a normal little boy."

"In Special Education classes."

"For now."

Parsons shook a fist, but kept his voice down. "He's almost eleven and behaves as though he were much younger!"

"He got off to a slow start and it wasn't helped by you trying to seal him off from the world. But he's doing fine now. And institutionalizing him would only stunt that growth."

Another grunted laugh. "You *like* that word don't you, Roy, 'institutionalizing'—you *like* to say I wanted to put the boy in an institution when you know damned well it was a school, a specialized school!"

"Live-in. Out of sight. Out of mind."

Had Parsons sat any farther out on the edge of the couch, he'd have been on the floor. "I will take this to court so fast your damn head will swim. I will charge you with endangerment of my grandson. You'll lose the custody you should never have been given in the first place."

Roy knew how to curl back an upper lip, too. "You need to understand, Alex—that 'creature' is indeed still out there, and he's trying to get in. If we remove Richie from the equation, the attacker may recede into the darkness and then turn up again when least expected. Right now we have a shot at stopping and catching him."

"You're insane," Parson said, his voice quiet but trembling. "I will not allow you to use my grandson as *bait* for this killer."

"You're right that we're dealing with a killer. Three other doctors murdered, and his note threatens both Richie and me. Hiding Richie away won't stop this fiend from pursuing his twisted goal."

Helen had said nothing as yet. Parsons turned to his daughter. "What do you have to say in this, girl? My understanding was that you came down here to talk some *sense* into this man!"

"That was before we faced this menace," she said. "And before I spent some time with Richie."

Richie, Roy thought. *She called him 'Richie'....*

"I thought you agreed with me," her father said, something pitiful in his voice now, "that the boy needed structure. That his imagination has a tendency to run away with him—that he can't tell fantasy from reality!"

Helen looked at her husband, and he knew she was

weighing it—whether to tell Parsons about her son's "friend" in the attic upstairs.

"He watches television," she said, "and he reads comic books. And he understands they are not real."

"You're on the side of this man who would use your son as bait!"

She shook her head once. "I'm on Richie's side. And if Mother were still alive, that's whose side *she* would be on."

Parsons took that like the verbal slap it was.

His daughter continued: "And if the moment comes when I think Richie and I would be better off elsewhere, under your protection, I will call you immediately. That much I promise you, Dad."

The father studied his daughter, and obviously knew her well enough to realize this was the best he was going to get right now.

He stood. Smoothed his expensive suit. Moved his neck around as if his collar were suddenly too tight. "You'll be hearing from my attorneys," he told Roy.

"Who knows?" Roy said, not getting up. "Maybe they'll do better for you this time around. But I don't think so."

Parsons was fuming as he headed for the door.

"*Grandpa!*"

Richie ran to him and took his hand. His grandfather looked down at him quizzically, as if the abstract problem of the boy had somehow inexplicably manifested itself.

"I have a new friend," the boy said. He gestured toward the ceiling. "Would you like to meet him?"

Roy looked at Helen and Helen looked at Roy, both white as a sheet. As a ghost.

"No thank you, Richard," Parsons said. "Your grand-father has to get back to work. That's what responsible grown-ups do."

The boy gave his grandfather another hug, which seemed to make the man uncomfortable, though he did again tousle the child's hair before slipping back into the sunshine, putting on his Ray-Bans to banish it from view.

Night had fallen by the time a '67 Chevy sedan got to the front of the line of cars at the roadblock that was swinging cars away from the stretch of pavement from which the Ryan compound could be accessed.

A broad-shouldered individual—with long dark hair combed back neatly, in a Georgia Tech sweatshirt that spoke of a powerful upper build—smiled pleasantly at the young-looking officer who peered in the driver's side window.

"Any trouble, officer?" The voice of the man behind the wheel was soft and rather high-pitched.

"Sorry, sir," the young cop said. He wore the uniform of the Sugar Hill PD. "You're going to have to detour around this area."

"What's the problem?"

"Just routine police work."

The driver nodded. "Will the detour take me around to the highway?"

"It will. Just turn right at the second intersection and follow the signs."

The driver smiled, nodded again. "Thank you, officer. Good night."

"Night, sir."

The next vehicle, a station wagon filled with a family, pulled up as the Chevy pulled away, its driver smugly smiling, knowing the angle and the dark would prevent the uniformed cop from seeing the specially installed push-pull hand controls affixed to the steering wheel.

CHAPTER 8

hief Blake Cutter pulled his Dodge Challenger up in front of an old five-story brick building in the middle of a wire-fenced-off block marked for demolition. With him was Detective Janet Hodges, on loan from the Buford PD. Janet had been working the phones, running down leads and gathering information.

The once proud building had a ragged hole in its face on the second floor. The structure to its left had several greater holes in its facade, but the work had apparently been stalled, and the two buildings to the right hadn't been touched yet. All of them bore the ghosts of a once vibrant retail block—store windows long-ago boarded up, signs faded and splintered, neon letters gone with their painted outlines on metal backing remaining...skeletons of commerce. In a lettering painted on the bricking between the second and third floors, the building with a hole in its face said, in very faded white, LEE & SON FURNITURE.

Cutter was off his beat, but not very far off—Timber Lake, Georgia, population 17,000, just north of Peachtree Heights and perched along the Chattahoochee River. A shopping mall, stables and golf courses kept the town alive.

Earlier that day, Buford PD Detective Janet Hodges—a pretty, bouncy brunette in her forties with a boy and a girl in high school and a husband who managed a convenience store—had corralled Cutter at the Peachtree Heights PD, in the chief's glassed-in office in back of the modest bullpen of desks and the counter where citizens could bring a beef or request or even report a crime.

With Cutter behind his desk, Janet took the chair opposite him and her bright eyes and cocky expression said she had something, *really* had something. She wore big-framed wire-rim glasses and a red pants suit with a yellow frilly blouse—a woman whose brains were matched only by her enthusiasm and girl-next-door attractiveness.

"Two of the three doctors our menace apparently murdered," she said, her voice a chirpy second soprano, "were somewhat controversial."

"How so?"

She leaned back in her chair, chin up, proud of herself and rightly so. "Samuel Carter was a pediatric surgeon who got himself in trouble a few times with the AMA—he used devices to straighten limbs, a painful and questionable procedure at best."

Cutter sat forward. "And we have a crazed killer who is apparently burdened with physical deformities."

Janet nodded. "We do indeed. And it's a similar situation with Lee Meyer, also a specialist in pediatrics, who isn't on the AMA's Outstanding Physicians of the Year list either—he invented his own version of something called a hexapod ring fixator, intended to try to lengthen legs."

Cutter's eyes widened. "A pattern emerges."

"Doesn't it, though? Now, our dead obstetrician,

Vernon Petersen, doesn't seem to have anything particularly negative or controversial in his past. But he *did* deliver a child named Dennis Chandler Lee."

"A deformed child?"

"The records don't indicate that, but Dennis and his grandparents, Efram and Rosemary Lee, turn up in the files of both Doctors Carter and Meyer, and always the same Timber Lake home address. Carter worked with the patient starting about two years after the boy's birth, and Meyer seems to have taken over perhaps ten years after that. Both physicians billed considerable hours 'helping' little Dennis Lee."

Cutter was nodding. "So if Dennis Lee was seeing a couple of quack doctors, thanks to his loving grandparents, he may well have been put through pain and misery and..."

"A living hell," Janet finished. "And as for the obstetrician, Petersen may not have been part of this torture team, but there is one other possibly significant fact— Lula Lee, the mother of Dennis Lee, died in childbirth."

Neither officer said anything for several moments.

Then Cutter said, "So...our killer's grudge appears to involve specific doctors, as we speculated. Does Dennis Lee turn up in Dr. Roy Ryan's records?"

She shook her head. "No. But we'll want to ask him if the name Dennis Lee means anything to him—don't you agree?"

"Oh, I agree, all right. Let me ask you something, Janet. Did you refer to our murderer as 'the menace' because his name is Dennis?"

She grinned. "I'll never tell. What now?"

"See if the Efram Lee family still has a Timber Lake address."

She was on her feet already. "You got it, Chief."

When finding a Lee family address in Timber Lake

proved a dead end, Detective Hodges had called Chief Wynn Sturgis, who had been evasive at first but eventually told her to round up Chief Cutter and come on down to his friendly little town. The demolition-targeted block Cutter's Challenger pulled up to was the address where Sturgis had requested they meet.

Cutter had been to Timber Lake a few times, as a citizen enjoying the boating and fishing, but not as a public servant from a nearby community, so he didn't know much about the place and had never met the local PD's chief. This block, off the town square, had obviously once been a retail center before devolving into an eyesore.

Chief Sturgis was stepping out of his own pulled-over police vehicle as they rolled up. Pushing retirement age hard, the beefy six-footer had a gut challenging the bottom buttons of his blue uniform shirt and two bushy white eyebrows that mimicked his old-fashioned white handlebar. He had big dark blue eyes and an endless smile in a walrus face, the kind of cheerfulness cops grew if the daily tragedies in this work didn't defeat them.

Next to Sturgis was a fit-looking Hispanic uniformed officer with a military bearing—that was the kind of haircut you got at an army base—and steady dark eyes in a deceptively boyish face. Cutter didn't know the officer, but the Timber Lake chief—after shaking hands with his visitors—introduced the younger cop as Sgt. Harry Lopez.

"First thing I gotta tell you, Chief Cutter," Sturgis said, as the four cops grouped between the two cars parked along the wire fence, "is we haven't advertised this thing. It's not a cover-up, mind you, but we don't need our little town getting a black eye."

"Understood," Cutter said. "We're dealing with a tricky situation ourselves in Peachtree Heights."

"I heard rumbles, but just rumbles." Sturgis's hands

rode his hips, his right above the butt of a big revolver. "How much do you know about Timber Lake?"

"It's along the river on one side and the lake on the other. It used to be a lumber town but that was a long time ago. A textile mill went belly up a while back. That's about it, I'm afraid."

Sturgis's eyes narrowed. Good-naturedly accusatory, he said, "You're not a Southern boy, I understand. You're one of those flatland foreigners."

Cutter grinned. "You've been misinformed, Chief. I was born and raised in Georgia. After the war I landed a job in NYC and spent a lot of years there. Lost my accent, I'm afraid."

"Won't hold it against you." Sturgis's head went back. "So you don't know anything about the Lee family?"

"Not even Robert E.'s." Cutter glanced at Janet. "Officer Hodges here said you were good enough to invite us down after she realized *this* might have something to do with the problem we're facing."

This being the building with a hole in its face.

Chief Sturgis thought for a moment, then gestured across the way. "Just around the corner, on the square, is a little coffee shop. Let's take a short hike over there and I'll fill you in."

"Lead the way."

They took a booth in back and a friendly gal in a pink uniform with a white collar brought everybody black coffee—not a sugar or cream in the bunch. *Four tough coppers*, Cutter thought.

Sturgis jumped right into it, like Andy Griffith selling breakfast food.

"The Lees," he said, "were wealthy and influential for generations, going back to the lumber days. But the family fell on hard times or, if not hard times, easy times was damn well over. Zachariah Lee, right after the turn of the century, started a furniture business with what was left of the family loot...well, they started out with caskets and moved into furniture. Any event, they came roarin' back. He and his wife Mildred had lost their fancy mansion on the bluff, but they lived like royalty on the upper three floors of that building you pulled up in front of, the one with the hole knocked into it."

Janet asked, "They didn't just build a fancy new place, with all that new casket and couch money?"

Sturgis shook his head. "No, ol' Zachariah feared losing everything again, and even before that he'd been a stingy cuss. When the Depression come, he felt justified and let everybody know he'd been right to pinch pennies. And he was richer than God—a director of the lumber mill, owned pretty much all the downtown, including that block you're parked in front of. Plus, he was the president of the Lee Savings and Trust Bank, which was not an institution known for its generosity of spirit."

"Not much, then," Cutter said, "for Christian charity?"

"Not hardly." Sturgis sipped coffee. "Oh, Zachariah was a Christian all right, or least ways called himself that. But more an Old Testament-type Christian. Quit the Baptist church because it was too loose in its ways and started up his own sect. That died with him, I'm afraid, in the mid-'40s, during the war. People needed religion, but not such a harsh, unforgiving variety."

Janet asked, "Any children?"

"Yes, him and Mildred, who looked like she walked out of that *American Gothic* painting, had three—two girls, who Zachariah ignored, and a boy, Efram, the youngest, who he adored. But Efram, who towed the line when his father was alive...kissed his butt, they say...had his own way of doing and seeing things. He was in high school when his daddy died and he inherited everything. Prided himself on a good head for business and handpicked the folks he put in charge while he went off to college in the east. Some say he bought off the draft board to stay out of the war, but people talk. Anyway, he came back with a law degree and a very beautiful bride, only she was an east-coast society gal, full of herself."

Janet said, "Surely *she* didn't want to live over a furniture store."

"I don't suppose so," Sturgis admitted. "But one of those smart boys Ef put in charge of the bank kinda helped himself to unsecured loans, shall we say, and the bank went under. Folks knew Ef had been swindled and didn't hold it against him. Anyway, it didn't hurt his furniture business any. People were setting up house after the war and business was booming just the way babies were."

Cutter said, "But not booming enough for the Lees to stop living over the furniture store."

Sturgis nodded. "That's probably so, though Efram wasn't stingy like his papa, and they lived just fine. Traveled some. Cottage on the lake. That snooty gal of his, though, was a real social butterfly. Not that there was any 'Four Hundred' in Timber Lake...probably not even Forty. But Rosemary, that was her name, was a beauty and refined, and headed up every charity and such. They had one child, a girl, a pretty thing, but wild. She got herself pregnant."

For the first time, the younger officer spoke. "Now that *is* just talk. Like the rumor Lula Lee ran off with somebody her parents didn't approve of, or the sightings of her reported by vacationers over the years. But everything else the chief has said can be vouched for."

Sturgis added, "And her folks always claimed their daughter married back east. If so, nobody remembers her coming back home for a visit."

Janet said, "One rumor is true, anyway. The records confirm that Lula Lee died in childbirth. Her son was named Dennis. Do you know of a Dennis Lee connected to the Ryan family?"

"No," Sturgis said, shaking his head.

"No," Lopez agreed. "But...I think we're at the next stage of our story."

Minutes later they were again standing before the partially demolished row of weathered brick buildings.

Sturgis, gesturing to the Lee Furniture structure, said, "This block of buildings was condemned and scheduled for demolition about a month ago. The owner, retired attorney Efram Lee, had not been heard from locally, or anywhere else for that matter, for over a year, his little office shut down. And the furniture store had been out of business fifteen years."

Indicating the building farthest left, Lopez said, "That partially demolished building was where the crew started, and early in the process the crane operator's grip slipped and the wrecking ball swung too far right and punched that hole in the adjacent structure. A bad, stupid slip, but since that building was set to come down as well anyway, it wasn't considered a big deal."

"But as work resumed," Sturgis said, "a stench rising from that accidental hole had the demolition crew refusing to work. They should have called us in, or at least put on masks before going in. But some wiseacres went ahead and battered their way in with sledgehammers and, for their trouble, got hit with a smell that cops like us know all too well."

"Death," Lopez said.

Cutter exchanged glances with the female detective, then asked, "What did they find in there?"

Sturgis said, "On the third floor, where the residence began, three bodies. Two middle-aged adults, in their late fifties, and a woman about forty. Battered to death and then dismembered."

Janet gasped.

Cutter asked, "Dismembered for disposal?"

The local chief shook his head. "No, the body parts were all there, scattered around willy nilly. It was more a random, savage display—somebody attacking the dead bodies after making them that way, maybe because killing them had simply not been enough. Because his rage was not fully spent."

"My God," Janet said.

Lopez said, "We identified the dead as Efram Lee and his wife Rosemary, and a practical nurse named Loretta Dornan—unlicensed and with a wretched record."

Sturgis flipped a hand toward the building in question. "We can go in and take a look...oh, it's pretty well aired out, and the deceased carted away. We can provide crime scene photos if you want the full effect."

"I should have those," Cutter said, damn near shuddering. "But for now, we better take the tour."

The first two floors were empty of anything but dirt, dust and detritus. The second floor, of course, had the gaping, sunlight-bleeding hole a slip of the wrecking ball had created. An old service elevator at the rear was not functioning, not that anyone had been tempted to use it; stairs at the back took them up a flight to where a musty odor of murder awaited.

The stench of death may have been gone but the bouquet lingered. Janet covered her face with a handkerchief, and Cutter was tempted to do the same. But something made him want to embrace the sense that death was still in the air. He had seen things on the job in NYC that would haunt him forever—every cop working in that city, in that job, did.

But somehow he already knew he hadn't seen anything yet....

The living room furnishings had been expensive once, early American and really high-end maybe twenty years ago, not surprising considering these living quarters were atop what had been a furniture store and its warehouse. Yet the upholstery was threadbare, the wood nicked and gouged, much of it knocked over. Framed family portraits of long-gone Lees hung askew as if offended by what they saw, a large one apparently of a mutton-chopped Zachariah Lee himself ruled sternly from over a fireplace. Perhaps some of these pricey if neglected furnishings could have still been salvaged, but Cutter saw them as representative of a pervasive decay running throughout this entire structure.

This was where the attack had taken place.

Chalk outlines were everywhere on a parquet wood floor that had once been lovely and now was now scuffed and nicked and home to a bizarre jigsaw puzzle in the shape of body parts. Torsos with ragged joints and truncated necks were the closest these came to actual chalk body outlines, and big ameba-like brown bloodstains were splashed not just on the floor but on the wallpapered walls and even the ceiling.

Scattered here and there were weapons of a barbaric variety—an ax, a club, a butcher knife, stained with blood turned brown and even black.

Janet said into her hanky, "It's a slaughterhouse."

"Yes," Cutter said. "And this is the killing floor."

The other rooms on this level lacked the macabre melodrama of the space ironically designated a living room—no sign of anything suggestive in the kitchen except the open drawer where the butcher knife had been acquired. The appliances were relatively modern, again dating perhaps twenty years ago. Time had stopped here. Among other things.

The bedrooms were on the second residence level, rather austere but nothing remarkable or sinister about them. Faded framed landscapes and more family photos lent a haunted house effect. The closet of one bedroom belonged to a man, the closet of the other a woman. That husband and wife had no longer slept together was no surprise—Cutter hardly saw this domicile as consistent with enduring romance.

Another room on that floor was a home office with a roll-top desk and a row of wooden file cabinets; also a wall of legal books. The aura of this space was decades out of date. Another was a TV room with a couch and several chairs and a low-slung color TV console with a large screen, 24-inches anyway, and a built-in stereo for records and radio. Here was, apparently, where this little group allowed themselves some entertainment.

The top floor was something different. Half of it was storage, boxes and trunks and so on, and like the other two floors there was a bathroom, though this was not as nice or spacious as those below.

But the rest was divided between the nurse's quarters and that of her charge.

The nurse had a nicely appointed, cozy space with her own radio, television, refrigerator, hot plate, sink with running water, space heater, and a bookcase with popular novels. A doctor's bag on her dresser was filled with bottles of drugs and several hypodermic needles.

Janet checked the drug vials and reported to Cutter: "Sedatives."

Across from the quarters of the live-in help was a steel reinforced door that had been knocked off its hinges, powerful dents left behind. Sturgis led Cutter and Janet into the room with Lopez trailing after.

These apparently had been the quarters of the nurse's sole patient, though "cell" would describe it better. The dominant piece of furniture was a sagging metal-frame bed with a bare mattress where a heavy weight had lain night after night, an outline suggesting perhaps a heavy flat stone had rested there...again, if "rested" is the word. The bed was affixed with chained shackles arranged for the wrists to be held in place, at about shoulder-level. Chains led to shackles attached to the framework at the foot of the bed, apparently to reach ankles that were a distance away.

This room lacked the smell of death, but it retained the terrible perfume of excrement. Even now, a bucket in the corner buzzed with flies. The only window was bricked up. A pile of children's clothes, clean—XL labels on shirts, 4T on pants—were on the floor by a wall. Whether the patient could change into these or, after sedation perhaps, would get changed into them by his keeper remained a mystery.

But then so much did.

Sturgis said, "Somebody was kept in here, probably for years. That nurse was looking after the...well, prisoner....What *else* would you call him?"

"I'd call him," Cutter said, "somebody who finally got loose."

Lopez agreed. "*I'd* call him a captive who tore through that door, got downstairs, and ripped apart the monsters who made *him* a monster."

Janet, knowing the attacker at the Ryan compound was powerful but small, asked, "Wouldn't what happened downstairs take a big, brawny individual?"

"Brawny, yes," Sturgis said. "Not necessarily big. Take a look at the impression on that mattress—I make him three and a half feet and maybe a hundred-and-fifty pounds."

Lopez said to Cutter, "Take a look at this," and knelt at a place on the floor mid-room. Cutter wondered what that was about until the officer plucked out a fat knothole.

Cutter dropped to a knee and had a look. The view was onto the TV room. From here 'a slanted view of the screen could be had and certainly the sound easily heard. Any talk between the people below would carry as well.

"Imagine," Lopez said, "getting an education through a knothole—imagine listening and seeing and learning all about modern life on a TV tube, knowing what you are and who was keeping you that way..."

"And then suddenly," Cutter said, "you get free."

CHAPTER 9

The scent of the delicious supper Helen had prepared—pineapple chicken—was still in the air when Roy met Chief Cutter at the front door. The chief had called and said he had significant information for them, and wanted to come straight over. Roy of course said yes.

Barely inside, a slightly hyper Cutter, Stetson in hand, said quietly, "Is your boy around? I don't want him to hear any of this."

"He's upstairs," Roy said, frowning, "with your man Jackson, showing him around the work-out set-up..." He dropped his voice to a whisper, not wanting his wife to hear. "...and probably show him how his 'friend' is well-positioned to keep an eye on things."

Cutter managed a little smile. "Glad to get any help in the security department where we can get it."

Helen took the chief's windbreaker and hat, then asked if she could get anyone coffee and no one, including herself, took her up on it. She settled again in a straight-back chair with the fireplace—going strong now

—at her back and the police chief and her husband on the couch, the two men angled toward each other.

The chief said, "Doctor, does the name Dennis Lee mean anything to you?"

Roy shook his head firmly. "No."

"Probably a young patient. Possibly a little person."

"No."

"The parents, perhaps? Efram Lee? Rosemary Lee?"

Roy sighed, mildly irritated. "No. You have access to my files. My memory is pretty fair, but go ahead and check."

"We will. And now I have to share some things with you that you may wish you could purge from your memory...."

Roy and his wife listened in shocked silence to the report of what had been recently learned by Detective Hodges about the three murdered doctors, and by Cutter and Hodges at the bizarre crime scene in Timber Lake.

When the chief had finished, Roy asked, "If I'm understanding this, our attacker would be rather young, even now."

Cutter nodded. "We have the date of birth, which makes him twenty-one. Old enough to vote and to drive and, apparently, to kill."

Helen, a look of alarm frozen on her features, asked, "Do you think the poor child was *born* a homicidal maniac, and kept chained up by his parents for their own safety? And his?"

Simultaneously shrugging and shaking his head, Cutter said, "We're unlikely ever to determine that, unless we capture Dennis Lee and are able to question him. Of course, we don't even know if he's capable of speech."

"Why on earth," Roy said, appalled, "did these people handle their child in such a reprehensible way?"

"We can only speculate," Cutter said.

Her brow tense, Helen said, "Well, I wish you *would* speculate. Frankly, my head is spinning. You can't drop us into this horror show without some guidance...some professional interpretation."

"Any educated guesses," Roy said, leaning toward their guest, "would be greatly appreciated, Blake."

Cutter was clearly torn. As a doctor, Roy could understand the chief's hesitance to wade into the kind of conjecture that might come back someday to bite him in the tail.

"*Please*," Helen said. She was framed by the glow of flames behind her as she sat forward, her interlaced hands between her knees.

Cutter sighed and nodded. "We know from the medical files of two of the deceased physicians—Carter and Meyer—that the parents did take measures to help the boy. These measures appear to have been radical and ill-considered, and undoubtedly caused the child great discomfort...even agony. But they did try."

Roy said, "And this torment could have driven Dennis into a state of fury. And madness. Leading to the restraints that at some point were initiated?"

The chief nodded glumly. "My hunch is he was raised for a time in a relatively benign, even normal manner. From the glimpses we've had of him on these grounds, and the strength and agility he's displayed, Dennis must have followed a regular exercise regimen as a child, one he continued throughout his captivity, eventually on his own. It would appear that - later, when they felt it necessary to restrain him at night—he was during the day given more free reign of his little world. With no window and a steel door, why not at least allow him that small freedom?"

Despite the nearby fire, Helen hugged herself as if from the cold. "But a bucket for his...it's *horrible*."

"There was a bathroom on that floor," Cutter said. "My guess is that for a time he was led there by his nurse. But as time progressed, and he regressed into something less, or perhaps more, than human...he was treated like the caged animal he'd become."

"Why do you think," Roy asked, "the child's very existence was kept secret? Hidden away, like something in a gothic novel?"

A tiny shrug. "I'm afraid the boy's grandmother was *like* something, someone, out of a gothic novel—she was vain and valued her place in society, which is fairly pathetic in a town the size of Timber Lake. Why Efram was complicit in all this, I'm afraid we'll never know. Perhaps he felt the family had a reputation, a respectable facade to maintain. But there you have it."

"And," Helen said, a profound sadness taking over her features now, "the boy's mother was dead. Not there to speak up for him. To defend him."

"And possibly," Cutter said, gesturing with an open hand, "to a certain kind of twisted mind, Dennis was the 'murderer' of the mother, Lula, who was after all the only child of Efram and Rosemary."

Helen hunched forward again, folded hands between her legs. "The grandparents got caught up in a vicious spiral of their own creation—the less compassionate and understanding they were of their grandchild, the worse, the more animal he gradually became."

Cutter nodded. "Again, speculation...though the crime scene speaks for itself. But one thing remains a big, troubling question mark."

"Which is?" Roy asked.

Head cocked, the chief said, "We almost certainly know why the three doctors were murdered—two of them put the child through hell, and the other one delivered the malformed baby at the cost of the life of Dennis Lee's mother."

"Vengeance by definition," Roy said, "always has a motive."

"Right." Cutter looked at him, hard. "So why have you and your son been targeted? You have no connection to the Lee tragedy that we can find or that you seem to know of."

"'Seem to know of,' Blake? You think I'm holding back on you?"

"If you are, now is the time to stop doing so."

Roy's laugh was bitter. "I only wish that were the case. Everything you've told me is some kind of living nightmare. Nothing to do with me, and sure as hell nothing to do with Richie."

Helen's voice came small: "What about...jealousy?"

Cutter looked sharply at her and Roy winced, saying, "What? Why?"

Her shrug arrived in slow motion. "Perhaps he's jealous of the love and care you take with Richie. Perhaps he's watched us from a tree or some damn place and resented the normal father-and-son relationship you have."

Roy said, "That seems crazy to me."

Cutter, not so sure apparently, said, "And nothing else about this thing seems crazy to you, Roy? But even if Helen's right about the motive for including Richie in his threat, why is this poor twisted soul looking at you and your boy in the first place? There *has* to be a connection!"

Roy frowned. Something in his mind sparked. He asked, "What county is Timber Lake in?"

"Fayette," Cutter said, clearly wondering where Roy was going. "Same as Peachtree Heights."

Roy leaned toward the chief. "This is before your time

around here, Blake. But it was common practice for the medical examiner to be some local physician taking the role on as a sideline."

Cutter shrugged. "Still is. You looking for extra work, Roy?"

"No. But my father was medical examiner of Fayette County, for about fifteen years. Starting around 1960. Could that be the tie-in?"

The chief was smiling, nodding. "Sure could. I'll get Detective Hodges right on it. She's my little bulldog on loan from Buford. If anybody can sniff the connection out, she can."

"And you've looked at my records," Roy said, "but not my dad's. Tell her she can have full access."

Helen's gaze went to her husband. "Roy, knowing all this...how can we stay here?"

"It's better than being out in the open," Roy said. "And I'm impressed with how Blake is handling the situation. Anyway, with what the police working this know now—and thanks to that sketch of yours, Helen—it should be simple enough to find and stop someone who looks like that."

Helen shifted her gaze to the chief. "My father thinks you're using our son as bait. It strikes me he might be right."

"I can understand that," Cutter admitted. "But with our attacker, we're talking about someone who has lived much of his life in nearly total isolation. Yet whatever this person is...whatever a horrific upbringing has turned him into...his intelligence would seem to be well above average. Think about it! Looking as he does, thrust into a big wide world he's never experienced, he's able to hide himself. Here, at your compound, we have a shot at getting him out in the open with a world of firepower to take him down, alive if possible."

"Wherever we are," Roy said to her, "Dennis Lee will come after Richie and me. Right now *we* have the advantage."

"Doesn't feel like it," Helen said with a sigh.

Cutter took his leave and they walked him out, the couple remaining on the porch as the chief in his Challenger pulled out of the compound. Two officers on foot patrol were in sight, giving them nods and waves.

The night was cool and lightly breezy, a darkening dusk painting everything a watercolor shade of blue. Forgetting himself for a moment, Roy slipped his arm around his wife's shoulders, then said, "Sorry," and withdrew it.

She moved closer to him. "No need. Go ahead. It *is* a little cold."

"What we heard from Blake was more than a little cold."

She nodded, shivered, possibly for more than one reason. "Roy..."

"Yes?"

"Whatever happened to...us?"

"You want my honest opinion?"

She nodded up at him.

"We had it too easy, at first," he said. "Your father meant well..." That was cutting Parsons considerable slack, but this *was* the man's daughter. "...then when Richie came along, and he had those tests made..."

"You felt you had to stand up for your son."

"Yes. I know you love Richie, too. Good people don't always see eye-to-eye, even..."

"When they love each other?"

He studied her. "Why? Do we, still? You and I?"

She looked away. "I don't really know. We've been thrown into something the likes of which few...if any married couple...has ever had to deal with. So we kind of *have* to be on the same team."

"That's true."

She cocked her head. "People can change, you know. For the better."

"Maybe. But I have to be honest with you, honey. I'm not going to change. Not where Richie's concerned. And not where I see my life going. This *place* is my life. This little town. My little practice."

"I don't want you to change."

"You sure of that?"

She nodded firmly. "No more custody battles. We'll sit down, you and me, no lawyers..."

"No Big Daddy Parsons?"

"No Big Daddy Parsons. And we'll figure out what's best for our son. Together."

He turned her to him and looked at that lovely face and he kissed her. Long and hard and yet soft and deep. Then he smiled at her and said, "You smell so damn good."

"It's the pineapple chicken."

He laughed. "Do I need to apologize for kissing you?"

"No," and she kissed him. Shorter, lighter than the kiss he'd given her, but she did kiss him and something inside him blossomed.

"This is my favorite custody battle so far," he said, "and *by* far."

They went back inside, hand in hand.

Helen said, "Where's Richie?"

"He must still be up there with that cop—Jackson. You want help with the dishes?"

Richie pedaled and pedaled and pedaled some more. Finally he climbed down off the stationary bike. He had worked up a good sweat.

He said to Sgt. Jackson, "Not bad, huh?"

The uniformed policeman handed Richie a towel.

Richie had just treated his guest to a full run-through of the daily work-out routine. He did this for the officer even though he'd already been through it this morning. He was really tired but didn't say anything. He liked having the chance to show what he could do.

"Not bad at all," the officer said. He had a big grin. "I don't think I could do a work-out like that."

"You could work up to it," Richie said encouragingly. He went over to where he'd set his stethoscope on the weight bench. When he was doing his exercise routine, he didn't wear the device. But now he put it back on.

"What do you have there, son?" the officer asked.

Richie told him it was a stethoscope.

"You listen to heartbeats and stuff with it," Richie explained.

The big man frowned. Not mad but he frowned. "You didn't borrow that from your dad's medical bag, did you?"

"No, he gave it to me. It's an old one. But it still works. I'm gonna be a doctor when I grow up."

The officer laughed. "Are you, now? That takes a lot of school, you know."

"I like school."

"Well, good, 'cause it does. There's other medical jobs, you know."

Richie nodded. "Yes. I heard Dad say. Nurse is one. Mostly girls are nurses but there are boy ones, too. And some people at the hospital order things, he said."

"Order things? Oh...orderlies? Yeah. They're like male nurses, too. Sort of."

"Can I hold your gun?"

The officer's head went back. "Well..." he said. Then he thought about it. Richie could tell he was thinking by the way the man's eyes moved back and forth. "I suppose that's all right, but we should probably check with your mom and dad first."

"Or you could take the bullets out. Then you wouldn't have to ask."

The officer laughed again. "That's very smart, son. But maybe I should ask anyway."

"Even with the *bullets* out?"

The big man laughed. It shook some things. Then he emptied the bullets from the gun and put them in his pocket. They jingled. He held the gun out by the barrel with the handle sticking out. The boy reached for it. But the officer held up his other hand. *Stop!* Like the cross-walk at school.

"Now don't you point that at anybody," the officer said, still holding onto the gun.

"Okay. Even if it's empty?"

"Even if it's empty."

"Even at him?"

Richie nodded toward the mummy. The boy's friend was seated knees-up where the work-out space stopped and storage started. His friend seemed to be watching.

"He's supposed to be dead," Richie said.

"Not even at him."

The officer handed Richie the gun.

"Cool!" Richie said, grinning. He pointed the gun away from the officer. At the air-conditioner making noise in the window.

"It's not a toy," the officer said.

"It's heavier than it looks like on TV."

"Yes. That's enough, now." He held out his palm and

Richie gave the gun back. The policeman spun the empty cylinder.

"So *cool!*" Richie said. "Do that again! But wait a second."

The boy put the chest piece of the stethoscope over the hole at the end of the gun barrel.

"Now!"

Again the officer spun the cylinder. The sound was really loud! Like some huge machine with great big gears turning and clicking.

"You *gotta* hear this," Richie said.

The boy took off the stethoscope and handed it to the officer. The officer smiled and put the stethoscope on. Put the earpieces in his ears. Richie grinned as he held the device's chest piece to the end of the barrel again.

"Spin it again!" Richie ordered.

The officer did. Then the big man smiled and said, "Say, that's really something."

"If you want to hear something really, *really* cool..." Richie pointed over to his seated friend.

But then somebody hollered. They were yelling up the attic stairs. "*Jackson!*"

"Yeah?"

"Chief's on the horn! Wants you five minutes ago!"

"Be right there!"

Richie said, "Don't you have time to hear something else cool?"

"Not right now," the officer said. He took off the stethoscope. He handed it to Richie. The boy put the headset back on. "But I'll be here again tomorrow and we can pick this up."

"Okay."

The officer put his hand on Richie's shoulder. "But till then, kid? You keep out of trouble."

Adults always said stuff like that.

Richie watched the officer disappear down the stairwell. His footsteps echoed up. Then they faded.

Richie thought, *How would I get into trouble in my own house?*

"Boy," he said out loud. "Adults are dumb. They think just because somebody died they're dead."

Then Richie walked over to his friend and sat cross-legged before him. He said, "I was just going to show Officer Jackson how you're still alive."

The mummy said nothing.

"You *are* still alive, aren't you?" Richie asked.

The mummy said nothing.

"I better check," Richie said. He leaned in. He was right under a clawed hand but that didn't scare him. Or bother him. He didn't want to hurt his friend, so he was gentle. Gentle when he held the chest piece to the mummy's chest.

At first he didn't hear it. Then he tried a different place. Right against the wispy fabric. Then the heartbeat sound came. It got louder. And faster.

Richie smiled. He drew away a little. He had to duck under the clawed hand. In the dim light at this end of the attic, he saw something.

Eyes in the sockets.

Or anyway something gleaming red.

Richie said, "Yes!"

The mummy said nothing.

Richie said, "Someday they're going to listen. I sure wish I knew what you were thinking. But you probably only speak Aztec. Maybe you don't understand my words. But we understand each other. You *know* I'm your friend."

Richie got to his feet. Yawned and stretched. Two work-outs today made him real tired.

"Well, better get out of here now," he told his friend.

"If my mom catches me up here talking to you, she'll give me hell. Or anyway...heck. You know." He shrugged. "Language."

The mummy said nothing.

And Richie went down to his room to get ready for bed.

CHAPTER 10

Considering everything that had been going on these past few days, Blake Cutter was not surprised to be called at home and summoned back to the station. But he could hardly have anticipated Detective Janet Hodges's voice on the phone saying, "We've *got* him, Chief. I think we've got him!"

Cutter pulled his Challenger into his designated space alongside the old two-story building on Main and found Janet milling out front, waiting eagerly for him. She'd apparently got the call at home, too, as she was in a casual blouse and jeans and no make-up, her normally perfect curly brunette hair mussed. But her eyes were on fire.

As she led him past the civilian counter through the bullpen where only a couple desks were attended, she glanced back, throwing him pieces of information like breadcrumbs.

"Caught the guy at the roadblock," she said. "Fits the description to a T....Blood on his shirt, cut himself shaving, he says....Right age, features in tune with the Ryan woman's sketch....Enough so to get the officer's attention at the stop, anyway....Powerful upper torso, long arms, and no legs....Double amputee."

"He cooperating?"

They were in the hallway now, off of which were the station's two interview rooms.

"At first, a bit," Janet said, as they stopped to face each other. "He has no ID on him. Temporary plates, which we're tracing. Says his name is Bob Davis, and there's a bunch of those in the system, of course, but not amputees. He was belligerent when he was asked to get out of the car—a car especially equipped to drive from the steering column."

"Does he use prosthetic limbs?"

"He has 'em, but he moves around on his hands at home, he says, and he wasn't wearing the artificial legs when stopped. They were in the backseat."

"You say he was belligerent?"

Her eyes flared. "Anybody tried to help him, he took a swing at. He's indignant. Kept saying, 'This is the thanks I get!' Well, this is the *f-word* thanks I get...."

They went into the viewing booth behind the two-way glass onto the interview room where Sgt. Jackson was questioning the suspect, not getting anywhere.

Janet said, "He clammed up when we got specific about the doctor murders and the incidents at the Ryans."

Cutter nodded. "More cooperative, huh, when he thought he'd just been brought in for driving without his license."

Her eyebrows shrugged. "If you call taking swings at police officers cooperation."

The suspect was wearing a black t-shirt that revealed a massive musculature. His features recalled Helen Ryan's sketch, all right—round face, deep lines for someone in his early twenties, dark eyes, the kind of flat nose a boxer earns from taking numerous bone-shattering punches, crooked teeth, bushy black hair.

Seated there, at the interview table, the man's lacking legs from above the knees down was not apparent at all. You would never guess this was the individual who Dr. Roy Ryan had described as half a man. Nor was it the little person they'd expected. But otherwise he fit. He really fit.

Sgt. Jackson was saying, "You're not going to answer any more questions?"

"Not till my wife and lawyer get here," he said. His voice was a gravel-edged baritone.

In the observation booth, Cutter said to Janet, "I take it he's had his phone call."

"Yeah. We're not getting anywhere with him."

"He hasn't had anything to say for himself since he got a whiff of murder in the air?"

She shook her head. "Just that we're persecuting him. And when we're done embarrassing him, he says, this station's going to be a parking lot...and he's going to own it."

They strolled back into the bullpen, where Cutter said, "Well, that's our man. Obviously."

Janet nodded. "I haven't called the Ryans yet. Thought it might be premature. And, anyway, I figured you'd want to do it—you're the one who's bonded with the family."

"I'll call 'em," Cutter said, returning the nod. "I'll make it clear our guy is at least technically just a suspect. But they have a right to get themselves a good night's sleep for a change."

Janet was frowning. "Uh, Chief—before you make that call?"

"Yeah?"

She gave him a steely look. "There's something else you may wish to share with them."

"Oh?" Cutter said.

———

Roy was on one side of Richie's bed and Helen on the other, the father in pajamas, the mother in a modest dressing gown. Famous faces from TV and comic books stared down approvingly at the little family as the mother tucked the boy in. A cowboy lamp on the bedside stand was on, but the overhead light was off. The child still had the stethoscope around his neck, draped outside his covers.

The boy looked from one parent to the other. "Where are *you* gonna sleep tonight, Mom?"

"In the bedroom next door, just like last night."

"Dad, is that where you'll be?"

Roy repressed a smile and said, "Mind your own business, pal. Better give me that thing."

"The stethoscope, you mean? I'm not done with it yet." He started listening to his mother's heartbeat and she looked at him with a you-little-scamp expression.

"The stethoscope," Roy said, wiggling a finger. "Come on now. You might roll over on it and hurt yourself."

Richie didn't seem to hear that. "Mom, are you gonna sleep with Dad tonight, like you used to?"

She was trying not to smile. "Your father's right, Richard. That's none of your concern."

Listening through the stethoscope again, the boy grinned. "Jeez, your heart's beating fast, Mom!"

She flushed and gave Roy a look. "I wish you'd quit letting him play with that damn thing."

"Language," Richie said.

"*Give me* that thing!" Roy stripped the device off his son's head and set it on the bedside stand.

"You say 'thing' a lot," Richie said.

"I suppose so," his father said. "What about it?"

"Sometimes you say 'thing' and I don't know what you mean. Lately I hear you and Mom talking about some 'thing' outside and you get real serious. Like it's a scary thing. What scary thing are you talking about?"

"The flu," his mother said, almost snapping.

"Oh. You call my friend upstairs a 'thing,' too."

"That's different," Roy said.

The boy sat up. "Dad, when your heart beats? That means you're alive. Right?"

"Of course."

Richie pointed to the ceiling. "Well, my friend's heart beats. So it means *he* must be alive."

"No it doesn't."

"It does so! And it's beating louder and faster, too."

Roy sat on the edge of the bed and Richie leaned back into his pillow, his mother tucking him back in better.

"Son," Roy said, "I'm glad you have a good imagination. But I'm afraid I haven't done you any favors, not getting your uncle's gift out of here sooner. That's a mummy, an Aztec mummy who lived hundreds of years ago. I want you to stay away from it until I can get it out of here, which I intend to do tomorrow."

"But, Dad..."

"He belongs in a museum, where people can look at him and learn something about life a long time ago."

"So he's *not* a 'thing'—he's a 'he.'"

"He *was* a he—now he's a dead person. D—E—A—D, son. He's not a plaything, and not something to play pretend with. It's really disrespectful, Richie, though I know you don't mean to be. It's our fault, really."

"But he's my friend, Dad. And his heart *is* beating!"

"That's enough of that," Roy said, stern but not scolding. "Now, get to sleep."

"*Dad...*"

Helen was at the doorway now. "Let it drop, Richard. We'll see you in the morning."

In the hall, Helen rolled her eyes and said, "You're right—that boy *does* have quite the imagination."

"Most so-called 'normal' kids," Roy said, "don't have imaginations *that* creative."

"No, and that's a good sign where Richard's concerned. But an inability to tell the difference between fantasy and reality? That *isn't*."

The phone rang downstairs.

"I'll get it," Roy said.

"Come back," she said, "and we'll pick this up here." She slipped into the guest room.

Not a romantic send-off, but at least an invitation of sorts....

In the library, Roy answered the phone and it was Chief Cutter.

"We *got* him," Cutter said. "We've got his ass in custody."

Relief flooded through Roy. "You sound positive."

"Well, he hasn't been charged yet, but he's being interrogated right now. I'm going to join in."

Cutter brought Roy up to speed on the events of the evening.

"He's technically still just a suspect," the chief wrapped up, "but it's hard to imagine any two people fitting our killer's bizarre characteristics."

Roy's whole body seemed to relax. "Well, that's great. Wonderful. But I'd prefer it if, for the time being, you'd keep your people on hand here."

"Absolutely. Roy, they'll maintain their patrol until I pull them off, which I won't do without your blessing.

We won't let our guard down, I promise you...but you can rest assured that we *have* him."

"Fantastic."

"And," Cutter said, the tone of his voice shifting into a different gear, "we've found the final piece of our puzzle, I think...or at least Detective Hodges has. She's been going over your father's files as medical examiner. Seems ten years and a few months ago, he presided over the inquest into the death of one Julia Miller, a death he ruled accidental. The woman died after a fall down the stairs."

Roy frowned at the phone. "Who the hell is Julia Miller? And how does that relate to our 'puzzle,' Blake?"

"She worked for the Lees in Timber Lake. Live-in help. A domestic, supposedly, but really she was a registered nurse, and you don't pay that kind of money for dusting and dishes. Janet called Chief Sturgis and asked if he knew anything about it. He apologized for not mentioning any of this earlier. But everything he had about it came strictly from rumors—there was never a police investigation of any kind."

"Investigation into what?"

"The Miller woman's death. Gossip was there'd been an affair with Efram and some said wife Rosemary may have given her competition a push. Another rumor was that Julia Miller was blackmailing the Lees. Still other talk said the Miller girl had threatened to go to the papers or the police about something."

Roy settled into a chair by the phone, trying to absorb all this. "And nothing was ever done about any of it?"

"No. Just small-town rumor mill stuff, and at that point the Lees were still very respectable pillars of the community. But it's not hard to imagine a scenario or two, based upon what little we know."

Roy grunted a wry laugh. "You mean, like social

butterfly Rosemary *did* shove her husband's lover down the stairs?"

"A real possibility. But what about Julia being a more compassionate nurse than her successor, Loretta Dornan? Someone who treated Dennis better than his grandparents, and who threatened...whether for blackmail or humanitarian purposes...to expose not only the existence of their grandson but the escalating cruelty of his captivity."

Roy's mind went into high gear. "If Julia had been a kind presence in the boy's life, and Efram killed her for threatening an unmasking...or if an affair had led Rosemary to kill her competition, as you put it...*either one* would explain our menace's grudge against my father."

"Yes. Your father rubber-stamped the Lee family version of the death as strictly an accidental fall. That he almost certainly did so honestly, if mistakenly, would not dissuade a deranged Dennis from adding him...and then you and your boy...to his vengeance list."

Roy shook his head. "My God."

"My God indeed."

"You'll...you'll look into this further?"

"Oh yes. And Chief Sturgis is eager to cooperate. For now, however...like so much in this case...we have to live with informed speculation. Somewhat informed, anyway." A sigh came over the phone. "Okay, I guess that's all I have for you."

"Isn't that enough?"

"I'd say so," Cutter said with his own wry laugh. Then, dead serious: "Don't let the sad story of Julia Miller cost you your first good night's sleep in a while."

"Do my best."

In the guest room, Helen was stretched out in the dressing gown on top of the covers under the framed Hawaiian landscape she'd begun on their honeymoon.

She'd been reading *The Thorn Birds* and set it aside on her nightstand. The reading lamp was the only light in the room and it gave off a nice warm golden glow.

"Was that anything?" she asked him.

Roy shut the door behind him. "It was everything."

He sat on edge of the bed near her and shared with her all Blake Cutter had told him.

"Is it over?" she asked him breathlessly. "Really over?"

He nodded. "It's over."

"Truly?"

"I think so. Blake Cutter knows what he's doing. And he's put a damn fine team together."

She smiled. "Language."

He leaned over and kissed her. Sweet, not lingering, but very, very sweet. She touched his face.

"These things Blake said about your father," she said, "and how you and Richie may have got onto the grudge list...are you all right? Does it upset you?"

He shook his head. "Not at all. My dad was as straight a shooter as they come. If he ruled that nurse's death as accidental, he was either right, or just honestly wrong. Everybody makes mistakes."

A half smile appeared. "You're telling me."

He had half a smile for her, too. "I hope I'm not the mistake you made."

"No. You...us? That's something I got right and then...screwed up. We never really did have it rough before, did we?"

"Not like this. But who the hell ever did? Of course, your dad made it a little rough, when we moved in together. Pulled the financial rug out from under you."

"That little apartment off-campus was fun. That's where I learned to cook."

"And where I learned to eat your cooking."

She slapped him gently on the shoulder. "I got to be pretty darn good at it."

"You did. You still are."

She stared past him into their mutual past. "We hardly had any furniture. Remember? We couldn't even afford a bed."

"All we needed was that mattress."

They embraced. Kissed.

"Richie was right," he told her, holding her.

"About what?"

"Your heart *is* beating fast."

"Yours, too."

Then he was kissing her neck, slipping the dressing gown off her shoulders, and kissing them. She slipped out of the outer garment and revealed the baby-blue baby doll beneath.

"Who did you pack *that* for?" he asked her, eyes big.

"I thought I might have to bribe you," she said sultrily, "to get my way."

Then she pulled the baby doll over her head and revealed all that lovely creamy flesh, the flaring hips, the narrow waist, the high ribcage, those full breasts, so high and proud with their puffy settings for prominent tips— all of her just as his eyes and hands and mouth remembered. She tugged herself out of the baby-doll panties, gave them a toss, and he clambered out of his pajamas. Then they kissed and caressed and he eased on top her of and the mattress sang.

"*What's going on in there?*" came their son's voice through the wall.

They fell into each other's naked arms, laughing, and Roy called out, "*We're just talking!*"

Giggling, she climbed on top and rode him gently at first and then picked up speed till he rolled her over and finished her fast and hard till they had both shuddered to a stop, though the mattress kept on squeaking for a while.

"*I hear something*," the voice on the other side of the wall said, "*and it's not talking!*"

Roy looked at Helen and Helen looked at Roy.

She said, "You've just got to take that stethoscope away from him."

———

Other than the usual symphony of insect song and bird chirps, the night was cool and clear and quiet, not even any traffic sounds with the roadblock still in place.

Officer Fred Dickson and his partner, Officer Lou Rawley, were catching a smoke on the side of the Ryan house opposite where all the action had been the previous two nights. Fred had just commented that he couldn't see why the roadblock hadn't been shut down yet.

"I mean," the skinny officer said, "they *caught* the guy, didn't they?"

The report had come in on their prowl car radio.

"Don't bitch," his pudgy partner said. "It means we get some time off and these long hours will finally friggin' *end*."

Fred shivered though it wasn't really all that cold. "I'm just glad we got this weirdo off our hands."

"Personally," Lou said, "I wanna get a look at this character. See if those crazy sketches do him justice."

Fred sighed smoke. "You think there's any chance Cutter'll pull us off tonight?"

Lou shrugged. "Might. I mean, what's the point? What are we doin' hangin' around this mausoleum if they got the killer in custody?"

"Ah, it's not so bad here." Fred gestured toward the

attic window, no air conditioner on this side. "That kid's a hoot. Little live wire. And his mom is a looker and a half."

The pudgy cop tossed his spent cigarette sparking into the night. "Yeah, that Doc Ryan's a dope if he lets a piece of tail like *that* slip away."

"Be respectful. She's nice."

"She's *nice*, all right," Lou said, leering. Then he huffed his own sigh. "I better call in and see where things stand. Maybe we'll get lucky and Cutter'll call it."

"Don't count on it. He's a book man."

"Ain't he at that."

With a wave, Lou disappeared into the dark. A minute or so later, Fred dropped his smoke, heeled it out, and the menace called Dennis came down from where he'd been perching atop the wall and grabbed Fred by the head and twisted, taking him down onto the grass, riding him all the way. Fred was whimpering and flailing, but the flailing stopped when Dennis, sitting on the back of the fallen cop, twisted that neck further, in a sharp manner that the mechanics of the human spine did not allow.

The officer lay silent now.

Little noise had been made by either attacker or victim, just a crack like the snap of a celery stalk. Anyway, the dead man's partner was already sitting behind the wheel of their patrol car, unaware, with the door open and the radio tuned to the correct frequency with nothing coming over right now but static.

Time to take matters into his own hands.

Lou plucked the microphone from the dash, to call in and get the skinny, and somebody cleared his throat. The pudgy officer looked to his left and, for a moment, saw nothing. Then his eyes lowered to the small yet so terribly large figure, grinning up at him maniacally.

When the gun butt of Fred's revolver hit Lou between the eyes with incredible force, the officer froze before pitching out onto the ground, his murderer having to scurry backward not to be under the dead weight before it flopped onto the grass. Lou wasn't quite dead, starting to rouse, and the little man with the big gun slammed its butt into the back of the officer's head again and again until it cracked like an egg and bloody yolk ran everywhere.

CHAPTER 11

I
n Interview Room A at the rear of the Peachtree Heights PD, at 10:45 PM, Chief Blake Cutter took the chair across from the suspect, Robert Davis of Suwanee, Georgia, and his attorney David Dixon, who'd come up from Atlanta.

The attorney was a dignified salt-and-pepper sixty or so in a tailored gray suit and navy-blue silk tie that together likely cost more than Cutter's monthly salary. Dixon's eyes were the same navy blue as his tie, and his heavy black-framed glasses rode above a graying version of Rhett Butler's mustache. For a man summoned from home so late in the day, he could hardly have made a more intimidating specimen of the legal profession.

"You took my client into custody," Dixon said, in a smooth courtroom baritone, "at gunpoint, with no explanation other than to say you were holding him for questioning, the excuse being that he didn't have his driver's license on his person or in his vehicle."

Bushy-haired, belligerent Davis, whose deeply grooved face could work up a hell of a scowl, gave Cutter a beauty. "Who do you slobs think I am?"

"Apparently," the chief said, "you're Robert Davis and you live in the area, though not in Peachtree Heights or its adjacent communities. You were stopped at a roadblock, were uncooperative, and threatened the officers physically. And, yes, you weren't able to provide your driver's license." To Dixon, he added, "Which all adds up to our legitimately bringing your client in for questioning."

"Does it?" the attorney said. "My client informs me that your questions ran to matters of murder. Specifically, these physician killings that are generating so much speculation in the media."

"Who do you slobs," Davis said again, the bitterness hanging from his voice like icicles from a roof gutter, "think I am?"

"Suppose you tell us," Cutter said emotionlessly. "Then we can discuss your whereabouts on certain key dates."

"This," the attorney told Cutter, "will tell you who my client is."

From a briefcase, Dixon slid a manila folder across to Cutter, who looked inside at some newspaper clippings. Less than a minute passed before the chief rose and, taking the folder with him, said, "If you'll excuse me for a moment."

Cutter joined Detective Hodges and Sgt. Jackson in the observation booth. On the other side of the glass the client and lawyer were exchanging smug smiles.

"We have here a Vietnam veteran," the chief quietly informed his colleagues, "who, when his rifle team was ambushed, threw his helmet over a fragmentation grenade and his body over his helmet. Saved the lives of eight men and lost his legs in the process."

Jackson said, "My God."

Janet stood her ground. "That doesn't mean he isn't our man."

With a joyless smile, the chief said, "Doesn't it? He lives in Suwanee, where he was born and raised, he's married with two children, and is definitely *not* Dennis Lee under an alias."

"We don't know for sure," she said, "that Dennis Lee is our killer either. We need to question Mr. Davis as to where he was on the dates and times in question, and establish if anyone can back him up, and do our damn *jobs* here, however unpleasant that might be."

"Understood." Cutter sighed and started to head back out. "But perhaps you'll understand why I am less than thrilled about the prospect of going back in there and grilling a Medal of Honor winner."

———

Roy was back in his pajamas and Helen in her nightie, his arm around her as she cuddled against his shoulder as they lay there with the covers at their waists. The night-stand lamp continued to provide a modest golden glow.

"How does it feel," he asked her gently, "to have it all over with?"

"We could go again," she teased.

He laughed a little. "That's not what I'm talking about, you nut. I mean, having this damn threat lifted."

She smiled up at him sleepily. "I know what you mean. But I don't exactly feel, right now, how you'd *think* I might feel."

"Oh?"

"Relieved, of course. So very relieved, but also...I suddenly feel like I'm home."

"You *are* home."

She studied him earnestly. "Am I?"

"You are if you want to be."

She took a few moments before saying, "The other night I asked you not to go. Remember? But you didn't stay. You left me here in this bed, alone. You were punishing me for leaving you. You and our son."

A small nod. "I suppose I was."

She locked eyes with him. "No suppose about it. And you had a right to get even. But I want very much to live here in this wonderful old house. With you and Richie. I can paint here, and drive down to Atlanta to the gallery when necessary. But mostly be here where I belong—with my two men."

"Your two men would like that."

"And, darling, I have to be honest with you."

"You don't *have* to...but I'd rather you would."

She looked past him. "I think my father was wrong about Richard. About Richie. Granted, our son was premature and slow to develop, and I know he's behind in many ways, but in others....Is he really even a 'Special Needs' child at all? If he is, that's fine, we'll love him and I'll nurture him, I will nurture the *hell* out of him..."

"Language," he said with a smile.

That made her laugh a little.

His arm around her brought her even closer. "But, honey," he said, "Richie *does* have special needs. A very special set of needs."

Her expression grew curious. "Oh? What?"

"He needs loving parents," he said, "who love each other."

As he moved across the front yard, across the gravel apron by the front porch, Officer Jerry Haines—like his chief, a displaced New Yorker and early retiree—thought he heard something rustling in the outbuilding where the gardening and other household maintenance equipment was stored.

A raccoon maybe, he thought. *Or stray dog...*

On his way to the glorified shed, the sturdy six-foot officer—blond and boyish at fifty-one—passed by the prowl car that Dickson and Rawley shared, parked near the front gate. He found no sign of either one in or around the vehicle, a fact he confirmed with his flashlight.

That rustling noise got his attention again and he headed for the cement-block outbuilding, to the left of the house as you faced it, set back a little. Though he, too, had heard the radio dispatcher report that a suspect was in custody in the medical murders, he shifted his flashlight to his left hand and filled his right with his service revolver.

The moonlight made him notice something he couldn't quite figure out—two separate, not-quite parallel grooves in the not-recently-cut lawn, as if perhaps a pair of heavy bags—of seed perhaps?—had been one-at-a-time dragged through there, flattening the grass. These depressions led to, and converged at, that cement-block outbuilding.

Converged, actually, right up to the door of the big shed, a barn-red, paint-blistering wooden slab that stood ajar.

Genuinely suspicious now, he sent the flashlight beam on ahead, followed by the revolver in his fist. He approached slowly and, a few yards from that red door, called out, *"Police!* Step outside, *now!"*

Which, if he were talking to a racoon or a stray dog, he knew was a wasted effort and risked him making a fool of himself.

With no response, he pushed the door open and, from

the doorway, he dispatched the beam of his flash to take a look around inside. Initially all he saw were such yard-work and general home maintenance items as a rider mower, a spreader, rakes, shovels, hoes, coils of garden hose, and an aluminum extension ladder, but finally—stacked carelessly on the floor like those two bags of seed he'd imagined—officers Dickson and Rawley, belly down and dead as hell.

The shovel that swung into him broke his right knee and dropped him to his left and his mouth came open to scream but didn't get the job done as the next swing of the shovel flattened his features in a bone-crunching, tooth-shattering *smunch*, knocking him back outside, onto his back, the face looking up at the moon barely a face at all.

Then two powerful hands took one ankle each and dragged the dead cop inside with the others.

———

Their Medal of Honor-winning suspect had been out of state during two of the murders—those of Doctors Carter and Petersen—and Davis and his wife had been entertaining some old service buddies at the time that Molotov cocktail had come crashing through the window at the Ryan place. That he had no alibi for the Petersen killing seemed moot.

They released him before midnight, but as he was going out, Davis—ever belligerent—said, "I don't suppose there's a chance in hell you people have found my car."

They were in the small lobby area on the other side of the civilian counter. Davis and his pretty, petite wife—who'd married him before he went into the service and who had stuck by him after—were just about to go out, their attorney acting as a high-priced doorman, possibly on Uncle Sam's dime. The loving wife, vaguely embarrassed by her husband's behavior, had fetched his artificial legs, which he now wore, putting him nose-to-nose with the chief—uncomfortably so.

"What do you mean, Mr. Davis?" Cutter said, working to be polite. This guy was a verified hero but also a certified pain in the ass. "You were *driving* your car."

Davis held up two fingers and it wasn't a peace sign. "I have *two* cars. Imagine that? One of them was stolen over a month ago and I reported it. Don't you cops keep track of such things?"

"We've been rather focused elsewhere," Cutter said, "and I would assume you reported it to the Suwanee PD."

"That's right. That's where I live! Where else would I report it?"

"Sir, there are dozens of suburbs around Atlanta, and as many departments. And, really, locating a stolen car is more the province of the Georgia State Patrol."

"Well, it shouldn't be so damn hard to find! How many '67 Chevy sedans like that are out there, anyway?"

"Like what?"

"Rigged up like mine! With hand controls." Davis threw his hands in the air, to make his point. "You people are unbelievable."

Then the little group was gone, though their former suspect's grumbling could be heard trailing off.

Cutter turned to Janet Hodges at his side. "Huh. His car was stolen. Do you think Dennis Lee might be driving it?"

"Who would have taught *him* to drive?"

"Good question. Maybe nobody. Maybe in the middle of the night he managed to get that buggy as far as a parking lot till he familiarized himself with those hand controls. Makes him mobile."

Jackson came up from the mostly empty bullpen with a slip of paper. "Chief, a call came in for you while you were in the interview room. From Chief Sturgis in Timber Lake. Wants to talk to you yet tonight, if possible."

"Wonder what rates that," Cutter said.

He brought Janet along to his office and made the call, which he put on speaker, then settled behind his desk. "Am I getting back to you too late, Wynn?"

"Not at all, son," the familiar folksy voice said. "I just called half an hour ago, and it's a good chance we'll be here at the scene a while yet. Maybe all night."

Cutter exchanged glances with Janet, then asked, "You're at a crime scene?"

"Not sure what you'd call it. We got a call from the owner of a cottage 'long the Chattahoochee. Lights were on in a neighboring place that's been boarded up since last year. Seemed like suspicious activity to this neighbor. Guy was surprised the electricity was still on, which actually it wasn't—but a generator was. But here's the prize in the CrackerJax—cottage belonged to the late Efram Lee."

"And you just learned Lee had a cottage now?"

"Afraid so. It wasn't listed in his estate. A kind of off-the-books deal. I'm guessing it was a love nest—maybe for him and that little gal who took a fall down the stairs ten years ago or so."

"You're at the cottage now?"

"Outside of it, at the moment. You're patched through to my radio in my cruiser. What makes this worth bothering you with, this time of night, is...well, I can't be sure if this bears upon your situation, but...somebody's been living in this boarded-up cottage. Somebody who knew about it from before, I'd say. Somebody smart enough to get the generator going and get himself some electricity."

Cutter frowned. "These are signs of recent activity?"

"Food in the refrigerator is fresh enough. Bed slept in. Soap and toilet paper stocked. We had two convenience stores get robbed in middle of the night. Looks like somebody goes shopping when the larder gets thin."

Janet spoke up. "Detective Hodges here, Chief Sturgis. My husband's convenience store was robbed last week, which is an embarrassment to his policewoman wife."

"You may get the chance to do somethin' about that," Sturgis's voice said. "Because I think your hubby's thief and ours may both be named Dennis Lee....What do you think, Chief Cutter?"

"I think," Cutter said, on his feet, "I told some people they're safe and they really, really aren't."

———

Officer Ben Raymond, another of Cutter's NYPD early retirement pals, was the last officer standing at the Ryan compound, though he wasn't aware of that. Sixty-two, bald as a grape, paunchy but still tough and alert, he knew finding that ladder leaned up under the attic window meant trouble. This was the opposite side of the house from where the previous assaults had been, but that just meant their attacker was smart enough to mix things up.

It also meant the suspect at the Peachtree Heights station was almost certainly not their man, as that ladder hadn't been positioned there on his last circuit of the house.

Service revolver in his right hand, he got on his walkie and tried to raise any one of the other three cops patrolling the grounds, but got no response. He clipped the walkie back on his belt and got out his flash and worked it around the area, starting of course with the ladder. Their mean little man might already be up there, though the window was closed. So what? Dennis the Menace—as all the cops working the Ryan place had taken to calling their man—might well have closed it behind him.

Was that little bastard perched somewhere along top of that fieldstone wall, waiting to pounce? Raymond swept the beam slowly along its upper edge particularly, and—while no sign of the menace presented him/itself—the cut phone line dangling did. Had the thing shimmied up the pole like a damn lineman and clipped it? Holy Hell, what were they up against?

He trotted around to the front of the house where the prowl car he and Officer Haines shared was parked on the gravel apron. He needed to call this in.

He opened the car door and the ball-peen hammer swung and its flat head sank into his furrowed brow. He pitched backward onto the gravel, taking the hammer with him, and when the hammer was yanked away, the sound was a sucking slurp like a boot pulling out of thick mud.

But of course Officer Raymond didn't hear it, nor the grunting of the low-slung yet broad-shouldered figure that yanked him by the ankles and dragged him around the side of the house toward the maintenance outbuilding, making a third flattened path in grass that really could use cutting.

———

At the Peachtree Heights PD, Cutter didn't even get a ring tone when he tried the Ryan house. He called the operator, who—after about a minute—came back and said the line was apparently down.

Janet Hodges was at the dispatcher's station trying to get through to any of the police on patrol at the Ryan place. She came over to Cutter and reported that she'd had no luck either.

Cutter said, "We need to get out there now. Tell the dispatcher to send two additional units, immediately. Then come with me."

She did.

———

After he'd loaded the fourth corpse into the maintenance outbuilding, Dennis returned to the ladder and started to climb. At the top, the window was locked.

He broke the glass with the heel of his fist—with the four cops dead, all the noise might do was attract Dr. Ryan, which was fine with Dennis. Then he reached in and around and unlocked the window, slid it up.

And crawled inside.

———

The breaking glass woke Richie. He wasn't sure what he'd heard. He even thought he might have dreamed it. But then came more sounds—not loud, just something moving in the attic. And that only made him sit up and smile.

Was his friend walking around up there?

The beating of the mummy's heart had been getting stronger, faster. So that made sense.

He got out from under the covers. He thought about changing into some clothes, but then figured the *Six*

Million Dollar Man jammies would do. But he took the time to get into his slippers. And to grab the stethoscope and put it around his neck. Loose, not with the earpieces in.

The light switch was at the bottom of the stair well. He flipped it on. Then he went up and was kind of expecting to find his friend walking around up there. Maybe moving slow, with his arms stuck out, like in a movie about a mummy who wasn't Aztec that Richie had seen. That mummy walked really slow, although everybody ran away from it really fast.

Yet somehow in the movie the mummy caught up with them anyway. It didn't really make sense, but oh well. That was just a movie.

And his friend didn't seem to have moved at all. He was sitting quietly on the floor in his faded color collar and thin tunic like always.

"Sorry if I woke you up," Richie said.

The mummy said nothing.

"Can't sleep?" Richie asked, walking over. He sat cross-legged before his friend. "Me too neither. I think Mom and Dad are asleep, though. They were noisy for a while, but the last I checked?" He lifted the tip of the stethoscope. "They were snoring. Dad was, anyway."

The mummy made no comment.

Richie said, "You can't sleep either, can you? You're *okay*, aren't you?"

The mummy's eyes weren't glowing red anymore.

"Hey, you haven't died again, have you? You don't look so good. You look different. Maybe I better listen to you."

Richie leaned in, under an outstretched bony hand, and pressed the chest piece gently against the wispy cloth. And the heartbeat came fast and loud.

The boy grinned and the mummy grinned back.

"I *knew* you were still alive!....Are there mice up here or something? Do you hear boards creaking?"

The mummy said nothing.

"Must be my imagination," Richie said, but he was a little scared. "My dad says I have a good imagination. So there's no need to worry, right? Anyway, you're here to protect me...."

CHAPTER 12

hief Blake Cutter was at the wheel of his Dodge Challenger, siren going, portable cherry-top on the vehicle's roof painting the night a vivid red. Buford PD Detective Janet Hodges, in the rider's seat, was working the radio for him.

"The two units patrolling the grounds," she told him, "are still not answering."

"Damn," Cutter said.

Due to the alert the PD and their expanded staff on loan from various area suburban departments were on, Cutter had been able to quickly round up three patrol cars to make the high-speed, sirens-and-flashers trip to the Ryan estate on the northern outskirts of Peachtree Heights.

"They're only checking in on the half hour," Janet said, trying to reassure Cutter but obviously not all that reassured herself. "Probably nothing to worry about. They're just patrolling the grounds like they're supposed to."

"They missed the last check-in," he said. "Let's hope they're just screwing off, hearing a suspect's in custody. Smoking, standing around talking. Not...in trouble."

"They're probably fine," Janet said.

At least only a few cars were out at this hour, and those that were quickly pulled over and got out of the way of the screaming cop caravan.

"Probably," she repeated.

———

The heartbeat in Richie's ears seemed steady and strong. As he listened, he continued speaking to his friend, who seemed to hang on the boy's every word, even though grinning as if everything Richie said was very funny.

"If Dad would just listen," Richie told the mummy, "we'd *show* him you're alive! He doesn't think you're my friend. He thinks you're a Halloween skeleton or something. He thinks it's just make-believe, us being pals."

Sighing, the boy in the *Six Million Dollar Man* pajamas withdrew the stethoscope tip from the bony torso's chest and said, "If Dad would just *listen* through this, he'd *know!* And you'd be his newest patient. He'd give you vitamins and medicine and help you walk again. Then we could *really* be friends. You could tell us things about the first time you were alive. It would be *so* cool."

With a sigh, Richie slipped the stethoscope earpieces out and allowed the device to remain slung over his neck and dangling down, and got to his feet.

"If I were a doctor," he said, "I'd help you. If I were a *real* doctor, like my daddy. Right now I guess I *am* just playing. But I'll get Dad to listen to your heart beating tomorrow. I promise."

He took a moment to listen for that rustling again and didn't hear anything. He wasn't afraid. Mice or insects skittering around up here were nothing a boy his age should be scared of (he told himself). But if that was a squirrel or raccoon or something, he should probably tell his father and leave it for him to handle. Wild animals could have rabies, Dad said.

As he looked past his Aztec pal seated near the start of the storage area's center aisle, Richie decided he better be getting down to his bedroom. He'd never been up here in the middle of the night before. In the daytime, sunlight came in the windows at both ends of the attic, and that single hanging lightbulb kept the work-out area plenty bright. All the exercise equipment was kept shiny and clean, and his dad had mopped and scrubbed around. It had made that part of the old attic seem new. But the rest had seemed ancient even before an Aztec mummy had been added as a sort of guard at the gateway to all that junk.

Right now, though, harmless things in the other half of the attic were making shapes that didn't encourage sticking around. Gauzy moonlight turned some things—stacked boxes and trunks and suitcases and chairs and duffel bags and clothing bags and old wooden crates—into mysterious silhouettes. Others—like the artificial Christmas tree and the old horse-head rocker and a busted screen door and spider webs and open beams—wore shadows like spooky garments.

"I better go to bed," Richie told his friend. "I'll see you in the morning."

A distant siren made him jump, and the boy laughed at how silly he was being even as he moved more quickly toward the stairwell. But the siren was getting louder, and he paused. No, not just one—it was *sirens*. Was there a fire somewhere near by?

That was when he heard the soft, high-pitched voice.

"Where are you going, Richie?"

He turned back, frozen there. He looked at the grinning, seated mummy.

Had his friend finally spoken to him?

———

Roy was dreaming about Helen and their honeymoon in Hawaii, but Richie had been in it too, building a sand castle while his parents in swimsuits watched him as they lapped up sunshine and the foamy tide rolled in as seagulls cawed. But then the seagulls cawing turned into the gathering sirens he'd managed for a while to incorporate into his dream, and he sat up in bed, sharply, alarmed. Moments later—in part because of how he'd reacted—Helen was sitting up, too, eyes wide, ears perked.

"That's close," she said.

"And getting closer."

He threw back the covers. "I'll see what's going on."

Leaving the guest room, he went across to the master bedroom and got into his robe and, sockless, stepped into his shoes. Then he unlocked the nightstand drawer, taking out a .38 revolver, which he loaded up from a box of bullets also in the drawer.

Helen, in the doorway slipping into her dressing gown, nodded to the gun and said, "Where did you get that? And those?"

"Blake loaned it to me. I asked him to. He gave me a box of ammo, too. Don't be mad."

As he slipped past her, she said, "I'm not mad, I'm relieved. Those sirens are coming our way!"

"I'll go downstairs and grab a flashlight and see what the hell is going on. You check on Richie."

She nodded, paused and said, "I wish you had another one of those," pointing to the weapon, and went to see about their son.

———

Richie walked slowly back toward where the mummy sat near the aisle of the storage area. The sirens were screaming now and the window at that far end seemed to have been raised and made a pulsing red hole in the house. The shapes of the spooky storage area were almost glowing red now. Maybe there *was* a fire—and it was up here!

The sirens stopped.

Part of the boy was thrilled that his friend had spoken to him. But part of him was scared, more scared than he'd ever been before. He couldn't help it. After all, his friend really did look like a skeleton in a fancy collar and a wispy dress.

Richie did not get right up close to his friend, the way he often had before, and didn't sit down in front of him, either. Hearing his friend speak changed everything. Part of him had thought the mummy being his friend *was* make-believe. He hadn't admitted it to himself, but part of him thought he was pretending.

So he kept about six feet away.

"Richie! I said, where are you going?"

His friend's lips didn't move. Well, of course not. His friend didn't have lips. But the voice was coming from that direction.

And if his friend could speak, that would show his dad that a dead man didn't have to stay dead just because he died a long time ago.

Right?

"It's late," Richie said, nervous. "I'm supposed to be in bed."

"It is past your bedtime, Richie."

And about half-way down that center aisle, a small and yet broad-shouldered figure jumped out from behind the boxes and crates. The pulsing light filling the window was at his back and outlined him in red, leaving the rest of him draped in black shadow. He was no bigger than a child of four or five, but his shoulders were broad, his arms long and held out as if about to hug. His feet looked real big. Were they bare?

"Who are you?" Richie asked.

"My name is Dennis."

"You don't belong here, Dennis. You musta sneaked in."

"I *did* sneak in."

Dennis moved a little closer, still in the aisle and its shadows, though.

"Are you a kid?" Richie asked.

"No. I never got to be one."

"I don't understand."

Dennis moved a little closer.

"I never had what you had, Richie. A real home. Real parents. Isn't that sad?"

"It *is* sad, but it's not my business. How did you get in?"

A long arm flipped back toward the red-flushed window. "Through there. But I can't go out that way now. The police are outside."

"I thought it was firemen. I'm glad there's no fire. But why are they outside?"

"Because they're looking for a killer."

"Why are they looking here?"

Dennis didn't answer unless that smile was it. He moved closer. The light from the hanging bulb finally reached the front of him. His hair was black and frizzy and wild and long, his eyes big and black and bulging, his nose flat, his teeth crooked, his smile a grin worse than the mummy's. He was in a loose black shirt that hung down over stubby legs in black shorts with his feet bare and big, his arms and hands and feet like a monkey's. He looked squished.

"Richie, we're two of a kind, you and I."

Richie was backing up slowly. "I don't think so."

"I really have nothing against you," Dennis said, and he sounded almost sorry. "Let me make this quick...."

And Dennis ran at Richie.

———

On the porch, coming out the front door, Roy almost collided with Cutter. A policewoman in plainclothes, who Roy would learn was Janet Hodges, was just behind the chief with a revolver in hand.

"He's in the house," Cutter said tightly. "There's a ladder up to the window on the east side. And we've found four dead officers in your maintenance shed, stacked like cordwood. Dennis Lee is here and he's gone kill-crazy."

"Shit," Roy said, the revolver in hand and pointing upward. "Both Helen and Richie are in there! I sent her to check on him."

Roy took the lead as they ran inside and started up the stairway, fast.

"If he's after Richie," Roy said, "that attic connects directly to his bedroom."

They found Helen in Richie's room, trying to open the attic door, the child not in his bed, the covers stirred. Holding back hysteria, she said, "Something's jammed up against this goddamn thing!"

Roy put his shoulder into the door and it gave a few inches, then wouldn't budge any farther. They could hear the groan of the wood and something metallic on the other side.

Cutter put a hand on the father's shoulder. "Keep at

it. I'll send a man in with a battering ram, and in the meantime, I'm going up that ladder."

Roy nodded and tried again.

Cutter ran out.

———

A few minutes earlier, Dennis had charged at Richie and the boy backed up quickly into the work-out area. He looked frantically around at what he might use to defend himself or maybe put between him and his attacker. Then he kicked a barbell, right in the middle of its steel shaft, sending it rolling at the fierce little intruder. But the agile brute jumped it like a hurdle and came on ahead, terrible teeth bared, fists high and waving, like some attacking native in a Tarzan movie.

Most of the equipment was light and Richie was able to pick up the weight bench at one end and thrust it toward his attacker, who backed away from the boy's blow, but then grabbed onto the thing and wrested it from Richie's grasp and tossed it onto the rowing machine, bending the device into a pretzel of shiny steel. Richie grabbed up the jump rope and whipped it at the intruder, who just grabbed it and flipped it away.

Richie put the treadmill between him and Dennis, who came at him and, in so doing, stepped onto the rubberized surface. The boy hit the switch and took the world out from under the deadly little man. When Dennis landed on his behind, Richie laughed, forgetting for a moment that this was no game, and scrambled behind the stationary bike as his assailant came storming over, eyes wild, spittle flying, and Dennis grabbed the bike and tossed it, sending it rattling down the stair well, where it lodged against the door and—in what for the attacker was a happy accident—locked them in.

———

Sgt. Jackson was on the other side of that door now, and he said, "Something's blocking it—let's take this thing off its hinges."

"I'll get a hammer and a wedge," Roy said, and went quickly out.

The noise up there was clamorous and beyond unsettling. The mother looked at the officer and neither could say or do anything but join each other in frustration and fear.

Outside, Cutter was scaling that ladder, revolver in one hand making it a slower go than he'd like. Below, Janet Hodges held the ladder for him and watched apprehensively.

———

Richie was running out of things to get behind or to hurl at this small, unstoppable monster. What was left but to hide? He ran from the mini-gym toward the aisle of the storage space, hoping to conceal himself or make himself harder to catch, but before he could do either he tripped and skidded and almost hurled himself into his seated friend, who seemed to be an amused audience of one at this contest.

Instead he landed at the skeletal feet.

"Please," he said, almost crying. "Please, please, *please* help me. Protect me, like Uncle Pete said!"

He could hear Dennis coming, cackling with mad laughter, bare feet slapping the wood-plank floor, which creaked in protest. The boy closed his eyes.

And when he opened them, he was looking into his friend's eyes. Eyes that began to glow. Glow as red as that window had got when the police cars arrived.

And the mummy came to slow-motion life, rising on its ancient bony feet, and Richie could hear its heart beat loud and fast and louder and faster and faster and faster, and the mummy's bony hands reached out and clutched the menace's throat and lifted him from the floor like a nasty squirming and screaming child and walked him down that central aisle through all that spooky stuff and tossed him out the window, taking broken glass and wooden framework with him, his shriek like another siren in the night.

———

Dennis Lee flew over the head of Chief Cutter, who'd been just a few rungs away from that window, and reflexively ducked when the menace went windmilling out, long dark hair streaming, clawed hands seeking something to grip and finding nothing but air, the whites of his terrified eyes showing all round.

Then the ground came up to greet him, breaking the neck of a murderer and putting the tortured child within out of his misery.

CHAPTER 13

oy and Helen Ryan found their son, very out of breath, covered in sweat, sitting at the mouth of the aisle into the attic storage area. At his feet lay the pile of bones and mummified flesh and decaying fabric that had once been a proud Aztec, including the once-colorful collar signifying some forgotten stature.

Helen hugged her son, gently, but hugged him.

Roy took one of the boy's hands in both of his. "Are you all right, son?"

"Sure, Dad." He was working at sounding brave and doing a pretty fair job of it. "I knew my friend wouldn't let anybody hurt me."

"What happened here?"

"Dennis...that's what he said his name was...tried to kill me. My friend stopped him. Threw him right out the window."

"You *saw* this, son?"

"I saw it. I guess we won't need this." He tugged at the stethoscope still around his neck.

"We won't?"

"No." Richie pointed to the sad, shredded remains of his friend. "He really *is* dead now."

———

After hearing about the extent of his son's struggle with the bizarre assailant, Roy took Richie downstairs and examined him thoroughly. Then he walked the boy into the kitchen where his mother had some hot chocolate ready for him.

Helen slipped an arm around her husband's waist. Both were still in their nightclothes and robes. "How is he?"

"He seems fine," Roy said. "Physically, he's ready for those Olympics. A few bruises and minor contusions and that's it."

She frowned curiously, nodded to the ceiling. "What in goddamn hell *happened* up there?...And don't say 'language.'"

He shrugged. "Not really sure. You heard your son. His says his 'friend' saved him."

She shook her head. "That boy and his imagination."

Roy said, "Yeah," but didn't sound quite convinced.

Richie was sitting at the table in the kitchen having the hot chocolate his mother made him. Janet Hodges was sitting beside him, having a cup of coffee. The police were still active outside, but whirling cherry tops had been replaced by work lights on stands. Several ambulances had arrived for conveying the dead.

Cutter and Roy, at one end of the kitchen, spoke quietly.

"Afraid you're going to have us," the chief said, "and plenty other law enforcement under foot for a day or so. This is the most extensive crime scene I've ever encountered, and that's after working Manhattan for a lot of years."

"So how are you going to write this one up?"

"My official opinion," Cutter said, and he was having coffee too, "is that Dennis Lee died trying to flee the police. He realized he was trapped in that attic and ran, and leapt to his death. Intentionally. Or misjudged that ladder and fell to his death. Accidentally."

Roy raised a hand. "I have no argument with that." Then he whispered: "But any thoughts about what *really* happened up there?"

Cutter sipped coffee. "Two theories. Either your son protected himself, and he's 'remembering' it in a way that he can handle. Or..."

"That mummy *did* come to life?"

Cutter shrugged. "Any way you look at it, Roy...it never hurts to have friends."

Later, on the couch in front of the fireplace where the only flames came from the hearth and not from a bottle sailing through the window, Roy said, "Well, I think he'll sleep till noon. I've never seen Richie more exhausted."

Helen shook her head, the blonde hair a lovely tangle. "What did happen up there, Roy?"

He told her what Cutter was going to say, on the record, and he shared the chief's two theories as well.

Her forehead frowned and her mouth smiled. She began, "You can't really think..."

"I think," Roy said, "a boy's best friend is his mummy."

She laughed, shook her head. "You didn't really just say that."

"Well, his mummy *and* his daddy." He kissed her. It took a while. Then he added, "Welcome home, honey."

A LOST MICKEY SPILLANE STORY
—FOUND—

On the occasion of the 75th anniversary of Mike Hammer's first appearance in *I, the Jury* (1947), we are including with the novel *The Menace*, as a bonus feature, the short story "The Duke Alexander," which bears upon two key aspects of Mickey Spillane's storytelling career.

During our friendship—which began in 1981 when we appeared together at the 1981 Bouchercon, the annual convention for mystery fans and professionals—Mickey shared various things with me from his files that he thought I might get a kick out of. These included two Mike Hammer manuscripts, each of which represented the first third of an unpublished novel. As it happened, I would eventually complete both (*The Big Bang*, 2010, and *Complex 90*, 2013) after his passing.

Another partial manuscript he shared was of the very first Mike Hammer novel (*Killing Town*, 2018), pre-dating *I, the Jury* and never completed by Mickey, and the unpublished, unfinished sequel to *The Delta Factor* (*The Consummata*, 2011). Again, I would eventually complete those works for him, honoring a request he made of me a few weeks before his death in 2006.

Mike Hammer was, obviously, Mickey's signature character (his "bread and butter boy," as he put it) but, strangely, he never published a short story about his famous private eye, other than condensations (by other hands) of his last two Hammer novels. Though Mickey frequently published short fiction, none of it starred his most famous character.

On one of my trips to his home in South Carolina, Mickey handed me the "The Duke Alexander," saying it was something he prepared in the 1950s for Mickey Rooney (and indeed a notation on'the folder containing the pages specified it as such). I was astounded to find it was a Hammer story, but became confused when I read it, because it didn't seem like Mike Hammer at all.

For one thing, it was a humorous yarn told in a Damon Runyon-style voice Mickey never employed elsewhere. The crime aspects were minimal, and the dual identity situation at its core brought to mind *The Prisoner of Zenda* (1894), the swashbuckler by Anthony Hope that Mickey considered one of his three favorite books. The other two, in a similar vein, were *The Three Musketeers* (1844) and *The Count of Monte Cristo* (1844), both by Alexandre Dumas. Mickey's *The Erection Set* is a modern reworking of the latter, and the former bears upon the shocking finale of *The Three Musketeers* (also, Mickey claimed in his comic-book scripting days to have written the scripts for the *Classics Comics* versions of both Dumas novels).

And for another thing, in "The Duke Alexander," Hammer asks a woman who is *not* Velda to marry him!

Curiouser and curiouser.

As was par for the course, Mickey didn't recall (or at least pretended not to) anything beyond "Duke" being something he put together for Mickey Rooney...who would have made an offbeat choice to play Mike Hammer, to say the least.

The manuscript was difficult to make out—a faded mimeograph—but as the only existing (and unpublished) Hammer short story, it was of course worth the effort. But when I set out with my fellow Spillane enthusiast Lynn Myers to put together a collection for Crippen & Landru of mostly non-fiction by Mickey, we decided (for commercial reasons if nothing else) to include "The Duke Alexander."

The shape of the manuscript, however, meant a lot of educated guesswork was required. Both Lynn and I worked hard at deciphering it, and Spillane expert James Traylor took a swing at it, too. We all three did our best, and it was published as part of *Byline: Mickey Spillane* (2004).

Shortly before his death, Mickey asked his wife Jane to round up all of his unpublished material for me. Among these extensive materials, I ran across a different, earlier version of "The Duke Alexander." What I came upon was—*is*—a typescript with Mickey's own minor revisions and corrections in pen.

In this, the original version, Hammer is not the protagonist—which explains why the story as Lynn and I published it just didn't sound like Mike. The hero here is Joe Moran, who runs a small-town garage and is on vacation.

It's likely when Mickey Rooney requested something from Mickey Spillane, the former Andy Hardy insisted that it star Mike Hammer. In any event, in creating a version of the story for Mickey Rooney, the major thing Mickey Spillane did was substitute Hammer's name and replace the garage with the detective's office and swap out the small town for Mike's Manhattan.

As the Rooney connection indicates, for a good portion of his career Mickey was very focused on Hollywood, even though he said he hated the place. He had a genuine interest in producing films, starting with a (lost) Mike Hammer test film he wrote and directed himself in the early 1950s featuring his friend Jack Stang, an ex-Marine and (then) current cop. Mickey was also involved on the producing end of *The Girl Hunters* (in which he starred as Hammer) and the screenplay for *The Menace* indicates his continued interest in producing and possibly directing film as late as the early '80s.

With the exception of some minor editing (spelling, missing words, etc.), this version of "The Duke Alexander" restores the original, and demonstrates that while Lynn and I (and Jim) did pretty well guessing when the mimeograph got too faded to read, we didn't always get it right.

As for Mike Hammer short fiction, there is now a volume (*A Long Time Dead*, 2016), collecting seven of the nine Hammer stories I completed from fragments in Mickey's files. The other two are included as bonus material with the 75th anniversary Hammer novel, *Kill Me If You Can*, published by Titan Books.

For now, however, "The Duke Alexander" is (as Rod Serling used to say) submitted for your approval as the one and only Joe Moran tale.

Finally, we are including a second bonus feature by way of a rare Spillane excursion into true crime, published in 1952 at the height of Mickey's Mike Hammer success. Essentially a lost story itself, "The Too-Careful Killer" has not been seen since its appearance in the Sunday supplement section, *American Weekly*.

M.A.C.
June 2021

THE DUKE ALEXANDER

THE DUKE ALEXANDER

'm only minding my own business, see? I'm sitting there next to the window crouched down behind a magazine so the porter would get the idea and go away. All morning long he's been on my back, bringing me water, steering me to the diner and even shaving me. Yeah, he hauls me in the lounge outside the men's room and gives me a lather and blade job before I wake up even.

Sure, I slip him a buck and he says, "Thank you, Duke, sar." Then I go back to my seat with him standing so close I can reach out and touch him. Nobody else gets this treatment. Just me. The guy's got everybody turning around to look and I feel like a bug in the customer's potatoes.

If I go to move, he's right there with, "Somethin' I can do, Duke, sar?" and no matter what I say he does it anyway. Can't even comb my hair. *Duke, sar.* That's all the guy knows. I told him my name was Joe and if he's gotta call me anything, call me that. So what happens.

"Yes, sar, Joe Duke sar," he says.

What a train. What a vacation.

Anyway, like I said, I'm only minding my own business when along comes this bozo. He looks like a lampshade in a double-breasted suit that doesn't fit and waddles up the aisle like a duck. Every time he passes a seat he looks at the guy sitting there, shakes his head, then moves on. That is, until he gets to me. He gives one peek at me behind my magazine and his eyebrows shoot up to his hatband.

He shrieks, "Ah, you scoundrel...you...you brigand! So you think to elude me. You are contrariwise! He who is the retiree from the Sûreté. Now I have you caught flat-footed and never will you get away again until you pay me my moneys!"

What can a guy do in a situation like that?

I yell, "Scram, ya bum, before I brain ya!"

Yeah, I was pretty mad. Does he flinch? Nix...not a bit. He perches his hands on his hips and taps his foot impatiently.

After a couple of "humphs," he says, "No... do not tell me. This time it is that you have the amnesia. You do not fool me, for I, Alfred, *know* who you are. Now, do I get my moneys?"

"No," I tell him, good and loud.

He smacks his lips a few times. "You say no. How can you sit there and...all right, tell me why it is no."

"Because I don't owe ya none. Now scram."

"Oh, I am distressed. Overcome I am." He holds his head and shudders. "This country, she is mad. I demand payment!"

Real calm like, I tell him, "Chum, would you like a punch in the nose?"

I get a real hurt look for that remark. "Of course, certainly not. The thought is horrible to me. Why?"

"Because that's what you'll get if ya don't get outa here."

"Ah ha! Now it is that you will assault me. Very well, we shall see. I assure you that the gendarmerie will not treat the matter so lightly as I. You are practically chained to the wall of the bastille right now!" The jerk snaps his fingers in my face. "Poof! I go, but I shall return...then you will go, as they say in this country, to the hoosegoo!"

Then he stamps off down the car with his chin out further than Mussolini's, slightly forcefully assisted through the door by a shove from my buddy, the porter. Natch, old toothy grin is my pal from then on. I wave him over confidentially.

"Look," I whisper, "we got a Section Eight car tagged to this train?"

"Section Eight, Duke, sar?" His face is blank, so I circle my finger around my temple and he gets the idea, then he makes like it was quite a joke. "No, sar, not so's I recollect. Very funny, Duke, Sar."

So I shrug my shoulders and go back to my mag. It's only ten minutes before we get to Washington, where I change to the Great Southern Special, then I'll be out of this rolling booby hatch.

That's what I thought.

I had a half-hour layover so I walk up to the reservation desk to see if I can do any good about getting myself a bunk for the night instead of doing my sleeping at right angles to myself.

Do any good? Man, the guy at the desk gives me a pair of wide eyes, then all of a sudden I am with what amounts to the presidential suite on wheels. He's all splutters and spluts, so I don't get half what he's talking about. But I sign my name, he gives me a very knowing smile like he's been let in on a state secret, and the merry-go-round starts to twirl again.

What a vacation!

Two porters grab my bags and zip off, but instead of

following them, I duck into a normal looking place where a bored babe in gingham slides me a plate of bacon and eggs, no questions asked, and I get some of my strength back.

I shouldn't've taken so long to eat. Before I know it I hear my train being announced and I rip out of there on the double. You know what the squeeze is like in a train station. Sixty-five people trying to get through a four-foot doorway at the same time. That's where they got the name bottleneck—opening the gates is like pulling the cork. Everybody jams together, then *pop*...they get blown through. Sometimes they lose their clothes, sometimes their baggage. Just as I was compressed into the breech I thought I lost my head.

A millimeter away I am staring at my own face! It takes one look at me and says, "Eek, I am seeing double! You are not me, so who am I?"

But before I can think of an answer to that one, someone pulls the trigger and I am shot through on the way to the train. Luckily, one of the porters gets me, or I would have ended up with the engineer.

At half past twelve that night, I pop straight up in my berth. I flip the shade up so I can see my reflection in the glass and say, "That you, Joe?" The image nods back vigorously, but I hold my hand under my chin just to be sure it's my own skull doing the bobbing, then try on a few grimaces for size. When I'm sure I'm not suffering a case of overdue battle fatigue, I throw my hands up and flop back to sleep.

Okay, now do you blame me for trying to get out of there on the fly when we hit Memphis? But do you think it did any good? Huh! Before the train has jerked to a stop, I am down at the wrong end, tossing my bags out on the platform and jumping for it.

I don't know what I expected, but it sure wasn't a

million bucks worth of southern fried chick in a gray twill suit, with a face to make you stop breathing and a figure to give you artificial respiration.

She has the prettiest little drawl, but the way she looks at me makes me feel like I just crawled out from under a rock.

She says, "I figured you'd have to come this way. Fortunately, Pam has a cold and couldn't meet you."

I try to talk but can't think of anything to say. Southern-fried motions with her beautiful blonde head. "The car is out back. Come along."

She doesn't need a leash, I heel perfectly. I'm far from being even a medium-size guy, but this dish comes to where I'd hardly have to bend my head to kiss her. She has more dough on her back than I have in the bank, but already I have ideas about keeping her in buckskins. I think to myself that maybe this isn't going to be such a bad vacation after all. When we get to the extra deluxe super sports special that she obligingly calls a car, I change my mind.

She turns her head and can't keep the sneer out of her eyes.

"I want you to understand something," she tells me. "It is three days until the wedding. During that time I'll do everything in my power to make my silly sister see the light and chase you back to wherever you came from. If that doesn't work, maybe a little violence will help." Then I get the world's nastiest look. "You'll stay a lot healthier if you take the hint now," she reminds me.

About that time I get my voice back. It isn't as strong as usual, but I can make a speech with it.

"Now, look, sis," I grind out, "ordinarily I'm a fairly bright boy, but I've been swinging at curves ever since I left home only hitting nothin' but pop flies. Just what in blazes goes on around here? I try to take a vacation and I get treated like a king, threatened like a criminal, then tossed back to the dogs like a college freshman at the senior prom. I even talk to myself face to face and that ain't logical. At first I thought it was me, but now I think the whole world is bats *but* me. Am I or ain't I Joe Moran with a little garage up in Holly Corners? Is this or ain't it a vacation where I'm supposed to have a good time? And just who the hell are you?"

Think that makes an affect? Nuts!

She says, "You can stop being incognito with me, Alex. I can see you've spent a good deal of time being indoctrinated in colorful American expressions, but for the time being you can put your garage away and just be sure that my sister is *one* curve that isn't going to be tossed at you. Incidentally, I'm Pam's big sister. You know —the grouchy one...Vi. Now let's go before the brass band Mother brought along finds out you've taken a powder. Daddy is waiting to have a prenuptial chat with you...alone."

So where does that leave me?

If I take off on my own, there is no telling what will happen. As least here I can put in a plug for myself if I need it. I like to know what's going on. Besides, I was getting ideas about straightening out some of Vi's curves. She sure could pitch 'em. I throw my bags in the back and get in the car.

We drive for about an hour without saying a word, and then pull up to a place that seems to be a small mountain with the top cut off. Part of the Great Wall of China keeps out busybodies, and the fancy sign that hangs on the post by the driveway reads HATHAWAY HEIGHTS. It should have been called Incredible Heights, because if you didn't see it, you'd never believe it. Moolah is written all over the place, from the crew-cut lawns to the mansion that peeks at me through the magnolia trees.

A small army of servants march out and surround the car. One picks up my bags like they were dirty socks and tiptoes in with them. When Vi gets out they all bow like the Rockettes, but with me I get a lifting of the upper lip and a nod. At the end of the line is the chauffeur who mutters something very nasty as I go past. That does it. I turn on my heel and walk back.

The guy has got one of *those* faces. For a chauffeur he's a grade A thug. Busted nose, thick lips and scar tissue over the eyes.

I say, "Punchy, did you just make silly sounds with your fat mouth?"

His hands fold into big hams.

"No, sir," he answers. Then as I go to walk away he mutters, "You'll get yours later!"

I'm a good guy, see? I can hold my temper just so long, and if I expect to hold it much longer, I have to get out of there. I look back at him over my shoulder and he must have thought I was scared, so he sneers at me.

Vi grabs my arm as I go up the steps. She is being very sweet all of a sudden.

"Daddy's waiting to meet you, Alex. You're going to like daddy, and if you want him to like you real much, you'll do just as he asks, won't you, dear?"

She melts my temper with that "dear." I give her a big, dreamy smile. "Why don't you do the asking, honey?"

Just like that she drops my arm.

"Louse!" she snaps.

What a shavetail! She gets over it fast. The sweet smile comes back and she steers me into the library. I've been in libraries before, and this one is just as big and just as quiet. And it has just as many books. Only the others never had a male librarian who looks and scowls like a bear ready to jump on you as you come in.

Before the bear can move, Vi says, "Daddy, this is the Duke Alexander. I'm sure he's going to be reasonable."

The bear stands up. He is even bigger than me, and like I already told you, I'm no midge. He says, "Am I supposed to bow or shake hands?"

I don't know what I'm expected to do, but if he wasn't Vi's old man, I would have plastered him. As it is, I stick out my hand.

"Ain't I pleased to meetcha," I say.

The bear shows his teeth, wipes his hand on his pants like I do back in the garage, and mitts me.

Right away I can see this is a game with the old boy. Vi smiles happily as his hand starts to crush mine into pulp and remarks, "Daddy used to be a steelworker, Alex. You wouldn't know it though, would you?"

I wait until Daddy is sweating a little bit, then step up the pressure some more.

"Really?" I am being real bright. "I never would have known it. I was in the game a while myself."

Then I look straight at daddy. He is getting red in the face and he plants his feet and gives it a last effort.

"Yes, sir," I say when I hear his knuckles start to pop. "Ain't I sure pleased to meetcha."

Daddy is real glad to let go of my hand. The old bear is a little on the cub side now, but his teeth still show. He drops in a chair behind the giant-sized desk and rubs his sore hand so I can't see it. Vi has her lip between her teeth.

"Sit down," he barks.

So I sit.

Daddy gets right down to business. He pulls open a drawer and yanks out an oversize checkbook. "I imagine you know why I wanted to see you, Duke. Ever since I've had a bankroll, a royalty-minded wife, and one foolish daughter, I've been keeping half the courts in Europe in cheese and crackers. Now how much do you want to go back where you came from?"

Well, it takes me a long time, but I am beginning to catch on. If I have any sense, I will spout off a figure, grab it and head for Holly Corners. But I don't have much sense. You can have fun on a vacation in more ways than one.

"Nuts, daddy dear," I grin, "I like it here."

Vi slams her palm against the arm of her chair. "Okay, Daddy, he wants to play it dumb. He won't take a cash settlement because he thinks he can marry Pam and get all he wants. Let him go ahead. Let him try. Just let him try!"

"I'll be damned if I will!" He is a mad bear again. "Do you get out of here or do I throw you out?"

The ugly chauffeur must be listening outside, because he comes in on cat feet. "You callin' me, sir? Want I should t'row the bum out?"

Mama saves the day for somebody.

I know it is Mama, because she is just what you expect to find in a joint like this. She bursts into the room leading a pack of people that must have been the local society, because there are more diamonds and fancy duds than at Tiffany's. Her face is a smile, from ear to ear, and she spreads her arms wide open and shrieks, "Why, Duke! You naughty, naughty boy! Surprising us at home like this, just when I was beginning to believe you had missed your connections!"

"Hiya, mama," I say. Then I squeeze her good. If they want an act, then they are going to get an act. It is about time I get into this game. Over her shoulder, I began to wave at everybody and they wave back. Some duck grabs my hand and pumps it. Two babes crowding fifty try to bow and almost split a dress. They get helped to their feet.

"But your voice, Duke...it has changed," mama says curiously.

"Sure. I got some jerk from Brooklyn to gimme lessons in American and now I talk just like people. Good, ain't I? Now I fit in."

I sure made a funny with that one. Mama clutches her bosom. "Why, how quaint! Duke, you're marvelous."

Vi doesn't think so, though. I see her looking at me, her face as black as a thunderhead. As they say in books, I am getting a look that could kill.

Not to get Vi and Pop in bad with the battle-axe, I dummy up a story as how I got off the wrong car at the train and was very luckily recognized by their charming elder daughter.

Then I spring the sticker. "But how's about Pam. Where's she?"

Mama pets my arm. "The poor dear has a horrible cold. But I'm sure she's dying to see you at once. George! Why didn't you show the Duke upstairs when he arrived? The poor boy has traveled thousands of miles to see his intended and you keep him away. Shame!"

Everybody snickers but Pop and Vi. They haven't got a word in edgewise yet.

Mama takes my arm. "Come along...son. I know you can't wait to see your beloved."

"You can say that again, Mom."

Her bosom rises and falls in a wind-tunnel sigh. She says to herself, "'Mom'...just imagine, having a real duke in the family."

I feel like adding "...at last" to her thoughts, because the way she says it, she has been trying for a long time.

Two maids are playing watchdog outside the door that keep Pam's germs to herself. They part to let Mama do the honors, and with a flourish she throws the door open and pipes, "Pam, dear, there's someone to see you."

With that she shoves me and I get propelled into milady's boudoir.

Pam is laying back in bed holding a frilly handkerchief up to her nose, blinking at me through watery eyes. She lets out, "Oh, Alexander, to think you have to find me like this!" Then sets up a wailing that brings the house down.

I say, "Aw, take it easy kid. You only got a cold. How's every little thing?"

"But, Alex, you're speaking in English!"

"American," I correct her.

Behind me I heard the door open a little, so I spread it on thick. "Ain't I gonna get a little hello kiss, sugar?"

"*You are not!*"

Vi comes at me with claws out, then remembers herself mighty sudden like. "Alex, we don't want you catching Pam's cold...not with the wedding so close." She looks at her sister. "Don't you agree, Pam?"

My intended wrinkles up into a sneeze and Vi pulls the covers up around her. She looks at us both very confidentially. "Now I'll tell you what we'll do. While you're recovering from the nasty cold, I'll have Alexander escort me around town and meet all your friends. Don't you think that will be best?"

"You...you sure you don't mind, Vi?"

"Not at all, darling."

"But...Alex..."

I say, "Don't worry about me, kid. I wanna get to know the lay of the land around here anyway. And don't worry about Vi here. You can trust her, all right."

I pick up Pam's limp hand from the bed and plant a smacker on her palm. "There's some healthy germs for you, Honey-bunch."

"Oh, Alex, you're so sweet," she says.

Vi mutters something I didn't get.

Mama meets us outside the door and Vi tells her the plans. I can see right off that Mama doesn't like the idea, but I tut-tut her objections and everything is okay again. Boy, this was the berries. With mama, the duke could do no wrong.

We take the tunnel entrance to the library where the old bear is camped in his den ready to pick my bones. When we come in he and the chauffeur, who are yappity-yapping at close range, jump back trying to wipe the smug looks off their pans, and I know that the *no-good* being bred had just been born.

Yep, maybe this wasn't gonna be such a bad vacation after all. Sometime during the day I had to get a wire off to my buddies who were expecting me at the fishing camp so they wouldn't tear up the countryside looking for me. Those guys were always pretty loyal to a mug who could never stay out of trouble.

The chauffeur takes off at a nod from Popsie and leaves the three of us there alone. The bear keeps an ear cocked for Mama's footsteps and growls, "Well?"

"Alex is going to be my escort for a while, Dad," Vi tells him. I can see the funny smile playing around with her mouth. "A sister's duty, you know."

The bear stares at me. "I'm only going to ask you once more. How much will you take to clear out of here? Name it and it's yours. I'm willing to go any price to make sure my daughter marries a man instead of a gigolo with a title."

"How about ten or twenty million." I wink at him.

His face got red up to his hair. "All right, Vi, escort the gentleman about town. Be sure he sees the sights. *All* of them," he adds significantly.

I don't even get time to change my shorts. Out we go,

not to the sports special, but to a shining black limousine. Parked behind the wheel is Punchy, licking his chops. Vi climbs in with me after her and the wheels spin in the gravel. Wherever we're going, we're in a hurry.

"Nice country around here," I observe.

"Take a good look at it while you still can see it," she pops back.

Right then I think it is time for a heart to heart talk.

"Look, sister. Set me straight on the rules, will ya? I'm having a swell time and all that, but leave us name some places so I can figure ahead of time. I've been climbing a tree ever since I left Holly Corners."

"Quit the act, Alex. I'm disgusted with you, your phony American accent and anything connected with you. This afternoon you had a chance to leave well enough alone, but you wouldn't have it. All right, take it any way you want, but you're not going to marry Pam if I can help it. We don't want your kind near us. Mother's title-happy and you're money-mad. Poor Dad is the one who has to pay for it. Pam will forget you in a month or so, but if we have to go through much more of these international affairs, Daddy will wind up in the sanitarium."

"But you got me all wrong, baby. Ya see, there's been a switch. My tag is Joe Moran..."

"Yes, I know," Vi interrupts, "you have a garage in Holly Corners and you're on vacation."

"Yeah, that's it. All along the line people have been calling me Duke. Say, who is this guy anyway?"

Vi turns and passes me over slowly. There is no doubt in her voice when she says, "Alex, although this is the first I've ever seen you in the flesh, so to speak, your picture has been staring at us from Pam's room clipped out of every newspaper society column for this last year. All I've heard since mother and Pam came back from

Europe is Alex this and Alex that. You are a very clever actor, Alex. I imagine your kind must have to be. But it is no use. That scar on your cheek is not fake, is it? You got that in a duel, I heard. One you lost."

"As a matter of fact, cherub, I got it when some babe hit me with a flowerpot. I was twelve years old."

"And your eyes are not the same color, one blue, one brown. How do you account for that?"

"You mean the other guy's got sad-sack eyes too? Amazing!"

"....The same height, about six-one I should imagine. Yes, you even weigh the same, one-eighty."

"Two-oh-six," I put in.

"So you see, Alex, you don't have to try to assume another identity with me. You have too many definite characteristics. I know you for what you are."

"Aw, phooey," I say.

I am getting sick of it all now. I am just about to tell Punchy to take me back when he starts to slow down. We are way the devil out in the country, off on a side road somewhere. The birds and the bugs are trying to out-chirp each other and if I hadn't been sore I might have enjoyed the scenery. Punchy gets out, opens the back door.

"This way...sir," he snarls.

"What do you want?"

"I want to show you somethin'. Come on, hop out."

Vi smirks, "Don't worry. It will be very interesting —jerk!"

Now she is making me even madder. I climb out and Punchy takes a little path up the field with me behind him. When we round the bend in the trees, he throws his cap on the ground, gives me the old leer and snaps a roundhouse right over on me.

Poor Punchy, his timing is shot to hell. I kinda bend at

the knees until it goes over my head, then tap him like the trainer used to tell me to, right where it counts. Punchy does a buck and wing, flaps his arms like a crow then sits down, his eyes like marbles. I put his hat back on him and picked him up.

Vi comes running out to meet me. "Nick!" she yells. "What happened to Nick?"

"He was gonna show me something and he tripped and his head hit a tree. What was he gonna show me up there, anyway?"

"Nothing," she snaps.

Vi doesn't know whether to believe me or not. I stow Punchy in the back seat and get behind the wheel.

"You come with me," I tell her. "By damn, I'm going to have me a vacation and you're going to like it."

She slides in alongside me, but she doesn't like it. It takes me a half-hour to get feeling good again. High-tailing it along the open road in the fancy rig is something and ahead of me is the city. Yes, sir, I sure was enjoying myself.

That is, until I hear the siren come screaming up beside me. Two big state troopers give me the heave-to sign, but since they have me dead to rights anyway, I am going to have a little fun out of it. I tramp on the gas and yell, "Hang on, baby!"

Boy oh boy, what a ride it is. Vi is shouting at the top of her lungs for me to slow down and each time she hollers, I jump the needle up a notch. The police car is dropping away fast when I hear a couple of slugs smack the back of the heap. I'm allergic to bullets. And those guys aren't fooling. The turns save us. We have a two hundred-foot lead and bullets can't shoot around corners. Then when we hit the straightaway, I give it everything she has, and when I look in the mirror, you could hardly see the black sedan.

"You fool!" Vi says. "You'll kill us all. Stop this instant!"

"Why, chick, I thought you had nerve. Golly, if I thought a little thing like that would scare a red-blooded American gal like you, why I'd..."

"*Who's* afraid? Pam said you'd never driven a car in your life and I don't want to be run off a cliff by a crazy maniac at the wheel of something he's never handled!"

"Oh, there isn't a cliff for miles. Relax."

I don't slow down a fraction until we hit the city limits, then I lead a rat race up and down every street and alley I can find. We can hear sirens all over the place by that time. Every cop on wheels is cruising the town with an eye out for the limousine. I park outside a theater, grab Vi, and yank her out on the sidewalk.

"Now what, bright boy?"

"So we'll leave Punchy behind and he can tell the bulls how he was held up by a maniac, slugged and taken for a ride. Come on, we have a vacation to enjoy."

I pull her down the street on the gallop, and turn into the first place that carries a beer sign in the window.

But we don't get a beer. A miniature tornado jumps from a table and points a finger at me.

"It is you! So you think you evade your debts. Now I have you on the spots and will wring my moneys from you. *Garcon! Garcon!* Call the gendarmes...at once. This man is a crook!"

"Not you again, pally," I yip.

It is Alfred from the train.

"So," Vi howls, "they even chase you in *this* country to get their money back. Now you're in for it...and brother, will I squeal on you! You won't get back to the old country for ten years! Waiter, call the cops!"

He doesn't have to be told twice. When Vi lets loose, four guys detach themselves from another table and move to cover the doorway. This kind of response I can understand. I grab a pair of chairs and go for the roadblock.

If I could reach it, I'd be out of there in nothing flat, because the opposition doesn't like the way I am moving those pieces of chromed steel and leather, but a hundred-twenty pounds of southern fried chick take me out high, and a butterball of one-fifty name of Alfred does the same down low, and the opposition moves in for the pile-up. A referee in navy blue blows the whistle, and I go to the Black Maria.

I guess I am the only sad one on the trip to the station. Alfred smirks and makes faces. "Now even if I have to sell the suits on your back," he says, "I will get my moneys. Aha, you never get away from Alfred as long as I live. We shall see anon. Aha!"

"Aha yourself and shut up."

"So! You still insist you do not know me. Ho. So I will prove it to you who you are. Tonight you have a nice bed in the clink and I will have my moneys. So! Ho!"

"And I," says Vi, "will send you cigarettes. Nice moldy ones."

The cop at the end of the paddy wagon tells everybody to shut up. Which is fine with me. I need time to think. The wagon tears down the main drag, makes a right turn and brakes screech.

I climb out of the cage with the cop standing by, one hand on a billy, while the driver gives me the thumb to get inside. Vi is absolutely overjoyed. She is loving every minute of it. So is Alfred. He marches in to present his case like a bantam rooster.

The cops on the inside are collecting us in a group with motions to be quiet when from outside comes the most gosh-awful racket you ever heard. Somebody is yelling bloody murder, and a deeper, raspier voice is for the other guy to stop or be killed.

A whistle blows, two cars bang together, and women shriek. *Whoosh!* Just like that the doors bang open and I run in. No. It isn't me, but it *is* me. Hell, I don't give it too much time. I get smart fast. Right behind me is Punchy waving a club ready to bash out my brains. No, that *other me*'s brains.

It is all so confusing, but I am lucky. I see it all before anyone else does and make a dive for the water cooler just as the other me buries himself in the arms of the cop that is supposed to be guarding me.

Somehow Punchy is disarmed, but he isn't devoiced. He swears up and down that he will rip me apart with his bare hands, he will cut me into little pieces and make me eat them before I am dead.

Alfred starts to voice first claims on my body and Vi wants to call the undertaker right away, but the cop stops her. I don't know how the bulls manage it, but they get everybody in front of the chief's desk before murder is committed. This leaves me out behind the cooler still in a fog.

So I can take a joke. I have me a drink of water, pat the cooler affectionately, then find a side room to peek in from on the proceedings.

The chief is next door to a stroke, Vi is having a laughing spasm and Punchy is fit to be tied. But poor *other me*. I stand there watching myself shake like a bowl of pudding.

The other me cries out "*Alors!* Woe is me! I am entirely innocent, I insist it. Here I am walking calmly down the street when I am attacked by this...this *thing!* I seek the protection of the noble police and what do I find? I am incarcerated! This cannot be America. I will refer the matter to my consulate! I will..."

"You will shut up," the chief tells me. I mean, the *other* me.

Punchy yells, "He beaned me, that's what he did. Picked up a rock and beaned me, then stole the boss' car. He's a kidnapper!"

This is Vi's cue. Yes sir, she swears, she was kidnapped, right there in broad daylight. I was a villain, even worse. And what was more, I was practically an extortionist to boot.

At that moment who comes in but the state troopers. One look is all they need. Yep, that was the guy who drove the speeding car. Yup, yup. They had a good close look and couldn't forget a face like that, yup, yup.

The other me is up there screaming that it isn't so. It is an international conspiracy so that good American dollars can't be exported to the old country. It is a foul plot!

No kidding, I like to split a gut watching it. The only trouble is, I felt sorry for myself even if it wasn't really me out there.

Then more people come in. The mama bear, the papa bear, and Pam, the baby bear. One peek at them and the other me lets loose in a foreign language that switches back and forth to English in tones that imply Incredible Heights is a suburb of Looneyville and that all was off in the wedding department. Mama faints, Pam opens the dam and forth comes a flood of tears.

"So now the would-be duchess is cry!" the other me says. "Ha...never would you see the inside of a royal court. For your moneys I care not a pouf! So there!"

Papa plays it smart. He grabs me fast. I mean, the *other me*. He says, "Are you refusing to marry my daughter?"

"Of the certainty, that I am. Arrest me, torture me, I am unsway. I do not marry anyone!"

Old Pop just grins like a fool. So does Vi.

She says, "I guess that tears it, Pop. We can go home now."

"But *my* moneys, what about my moneys?" Alfred hoots. "Am I to be deprived of my moneys? Am I to be deprived of what is owed me?"

The other me gives him a haughty look. "It is a trifling sum. I will pay you someday."

"*Now!* I want it now!" Alfred does a dance.

Papa laughs. "How much does he owe you?"

"Three thousand American dollars....trifling sum, ha! It will take him all his *life* to earn that in the hoosegoo. How am I to collect?"

Papa shows him how in a swipe of his pen on a blank check. "It's worth it," he says.

Just then Mama comes to and faints all over again. Pam decides to stay out of it with a little faint of her own. Punchy fans her with his hat, but he keeps glowering at the Duke. By this time I am leaning against my door jamb, out of breath from laughing. Honest, this was the best vacation I ever had in my life!

Vi and the old bear put their heads together, then Papa steps forward. Right away I see he is a big man in these parts. His whisper is loud enough for me to hear.

"Chief, do you think we can straighten this thing out of court? I'll be glad to pay any fines or damages, and if you jug this jerk, there really is liable to be some kind of international complications. What do you think?"

I know that Pop is more concerned with the publicity angle than any across-the-ocean mix-up, but the chief saw the wisdom in the words. The matter is straightened out then and there.

While the Duke is putting his ruffled feathers back together, Vi walks up to him. "You know, for a while there I was beginning to like you. Yet you almost have me fooled. I couldn't see how anybody could pick up a

Brooklyn accent so fast. You almost, but not quite, sold me a bill of goods."

My heart does a flip. Then it flops when the Duke looks at her as though she were crazy.

"Silly girl," he sneers, and much to Punchy's disgust, stalks out.

I wait until they all stood outside on the sidewalk. Papa loads the mama bear and Pam into one car, while Punchy holds the door of the limousine open for Vi. The Duke is nowhere around. After Papa drives off, I came down the steps fast.

"Hey, chick, how about that beer we missed having?"

"*You!*" she gasps.

Punchy said something like, "*Agrrr!*" He came boiling around the car and sneered, then let loose with that roundhouse. I bend a little at the knees again and it breezes by, then I plant one on him, and this time he does the buck and wing on the other foot.

"That guy will never learn," I say to Vi. She is standing there with her mouth wide open, staring at me with those big blue eyes. When I take her arm and took off down the street, she is as limp as wet spaghetti.

I laugh because I get her point. She never saw the Duke dash in the station house ahead of Punchy. Sure— she thought Punchy happened to see me and came charging up to get his licks in while he could. Oh, great!

It takes a while, but we reach the spot where I almost ordered the beer. We sit at the table a minute, then the waiter comes up with a half empty bottle in his hand.

"Can't you stay put, Mac?"

"Who, me?"

"Yeah, you."

Then I see what he meant. The "Pointers" door opens and the Duke comes out. He is a sorry sight. Vi shrieks and stares at him, then at me, then back to him again.

Right then her mind is in an awful stew. I pat her on the head and stand up. After all, I do owe the Duke something.

I went over and held out my hand. "Look, pal, how about you and me let bygones be bygones. I'll..."

"*Eek!* It is my doubles again! You have ruined everything. Ah ha! Ah ha! Now you come to me on bend knee for forgiving. No is the answer. Nothing I forgive, not one little thing! You have made me look like a fool, and for that I am objectionable!"

His arms go wide and he shouts to the public, "This...this *man*, he has stole my train, my woman, my honor..." His eyes found the half empty bottle on my table. "...now he's even drinking the beer I ordered yet!"

"Now look, it was all a mis—"

"Do not 'now look' me. It was the insult supreme and I am challenge you. To the death we fight."

Up comes his hand and patty-cakes me across the cheek. All is quiet. I see the bartender reaching for the phone.

Right then I look over my shoulder at Vi. "Now do you believe I'm just Joe Moran with a garage in Holly Corners?"

Vi nods.

"Did you really mean that about sorta liking me?"

Vi nods.

"Enough to marry me quick so we can get out of this madhouse and up where all the nuts are on the trees?"

Vi nods.

My face is still stinging from that slap. I grab hold of the Duke's coat. "Okay, Buster, you asked for this, but remember something, from now on there ain't gonna be nobody what'll mistake me for you again!"

It only takes one solid punch to change the Duke's whole personality. His looks, too. The bartender is busy on the phone. I hear the siren wailing. I yank Vi to her feet and we beat it out to a taxi.

"Union Station," I order.

"Where are we going?" Vi asks. "Dad won't like this."

I grin at her, "I don't know about that, chick. He said he wanted a man in the family. Now he's got one. There's a train going north in five minutes and you better hope we make it. I don't think we can get your Pop to talk us out of anything ever again."

The taxi is in time. I pay the driver as we unpile, but I am slightly disturbed. Vi hasn't said a word during the entire ride to speak of. As we run for the train I give her one last chance. "Want to back out, honey?"

She shakes her head.

"Then why so quiet?"

"I was just thinking..."

"Yeah?"

The train jerks, starts to pull out, and I shove her aboard.

"When you socked the Duke back there, so there wouldn't be any more mix-ups...Now he doesn't look like *anybody*...but you still look like the Duke!"

A white-sleeved arm shoots out, pulls Vi up, then grabs me. I look up into the grinning face of my pal, the same porter that came down with me.

"Glad to see you back, Duke, sar," he says.

I let out a long groan. "Oh no, not again!"

Vi says, "See what I mean?"

I saw.

THE TOO-CAREFUL KILLER

THE TOO-CAREFUL KILLER

There's a penalty for murder. Sometimes the payoff isn't too quick, but it comes. Time can be a torturer and some place there's always a killer dying piece by piece, a little more each day, cursing himself when he's asleep and feeling his mind loosening when he's awake until he has to fight to hold on.

Then maybe he starts wishing he were dead, too. Or anything but alive and not knowing when his kill is going to come back and haunt him and hound him — and betray him.

Some place, on July 6, 1940, there was a killer and a dead body, known only to time. Then a killer's mistake came home to roost.

The man in the rowboat fishing Washington State's Olympic Mountains Crescent Lake probably knew the legend. The lake never gave up its dead, tradition held. The dead stayed dead, the dead stayed put in this icy lake fed by the near freezing mountain streams that bordered it.

So there was only curiosity in the fisherman's mind

when he saw the tapering fingers of a hand break the surface of the lake.

But curiosity can even overcome horror. He rowed closer, perhaps even felt relief when he noticed the waxy sheen of the hand, thinking it was only that of a window-display dummy. Then came sickish horror when he realized the hand was real and so was the body that hung there beneath it.

Tradition had been broken. The lake had given up its dead.

It didn't take medical science very long to give its explanation. Perhaps Crescent Lake never gave up the dead it claimed, but Crescent Lake had never claimed this woman. Somewhere she had been beaten and strangled and her killer knew of Nature's own tomb to bury her in. Nature wasn't enough, though, he reasoned. He'd insure his kill and bury it deep, his insurance a stout rope and a weight to lock the tomb's door.

It was his own tomb that he locked. If he had left nature alone, he would have been safe. Had he merely dropped the body in the water it would have remained at a level where natural decay and the attacks of fish would have disposed of it.

His improvement on Nature brought his kill back to life because the icy waters of the lower levels completely preserved the body, and during that time permitted a slow transformation known as saponification . . . chemicals in the water united with the fat molecules in the tissue to form soap . . . the floating kind!

Time had betrayed the killer, because the rope finally rotted, but the body had been a long time in rising. Pathologists established that the woman had been dead from one to three years.

Sheriff Charles Kemp, Criminologist Hollis Fultz and

Prosecutor Ralph Smythe had a corpse, and some questions. They wanted answers . . . badly. The natural embalming process had left the woman's face deformed so that photos were of no help, but there were other, more useful clues.

They knew she was young, pretty and unusually small waisted. Her right foot had a huge bunion. Scraps of the blanket she was wrapped in, shreds of the rope that tied her, clung to her body. She still wore fragments of a dress . . . but wore something more important—a six-tooth partial dental plate the killer forgot to remove.

Acting on this last piece of evidence, the authorities had 15,000 circulars printed and distributed to dentists around the country.

Photos and descriptions of the denture were published in newspapers and dental magazines. If the killer saw them and knew any sudden panic at all it must have gradually left him, because there was no report on the denture throughout 1940 or during early 1941.

Meanwhile, three dead ends had to be run down. Three women reported missing in the Crescent Lake area were identified as the victim and in each instance the missing person had identical measurements and the same colored hair.

The criminologists solved those cases but as yet could not identify their own murder victim.

The trio of sleuths worked another angle. Medical crime experts had determined that prior to her death the victim had had her hair set. In their opinion the bunion on her foot indicated that she had been employed in a laundry or as a waitress.

Here greater ingenuity than the killer's came into the picture. Edgar Thompson, secretary and treasurer of the Culinary Alliance, came up with names of several women who had dropped out of the organization during the time in question. One had done a peculiar thing. . .she had left without taking a union transfer or withdrawal card,

Her name was Hallie Illingworth.

With this information the lawmen located Hallie's married sister, Lois Bailie, in Walla Walla, Washington, to confirm their identification. Mrs. Bailie reported that her sister had been missing since a few days before Christmas 1937; she did have a partial denture in her upper jaw and an agonizing bunion on her right foot.

What was more important, she said Hallie Illingworth had a husband, Monty, who claimed Hallie had walked out on him for a naval officer, then later she was some place in Alaska. . .and Monty wasn't around to say differently. At that time his address was unknown.

When the trail is hot the hounds run faster. The police moved into Vancouver, Washington, for a short talk with another sister of the missing Hallie, Mrs. James Johnson. Two more pieces dropped into place, Mrs. Johnson established the date when Hallie was last heard from with a postcard dated December 21, 1937, from Port Angeles, Washington, and also led them to the dentist, Dr. A. J. McDowell of Faulkton, South Dakota, who identified his handiwork in Hallie's partial plate.

Some place a killer must have been getting mighty nervous.

———

There was still another path in this rat race with a murderer. A path that took the officers to a cook house in a lumber camp at Lake Pleasant near Port Angeles. At its end was Jessie Hudson, a friend of Hallie, and she had a story to tell, one of intense jealousy between Monty and Hallie that brought on constant fights. A story that linked Monty with a girl named Elinore Pearson and set the stage for the final act.

The evil that murder is rooted in can't slay hidden long. Now the officers knew what tack to take. They began to find out things about Monty and Hallie Illing-worth. More than once Hallie had said that if they didn't separate one would kill the other. And once a hotel owner had entered their room at the sound of fighting and found Monty standing over Hallie, who lay moaning on the bed.

So the finger swung to Monty. He had, it developed, been granted an uncontested divorce from Hallie in 1938 at the very time her body lay weighted in Crescent Lake!

Monty, a 32-year-old truck driver, was located living with Elinore Pearson in Long Beach, California. He gave some confusing statements and then, when he realized he was trapped, began to tell a story with some logic. He said that on the night of December 21 he went to a party with a friend, Tony Enos. They were out all night. When he came home the next day, drunk and boisterous, Hallie was angry. She left the house, he said, swearing she would never return.

Police located Tony Enos. He confirmed the party and the date. He said he had brought Monty home at 3:30 a.m., and had seen him again at 9 a.m. near a Port Angeles bank. Monty, Enos said, told him he was taking Hallie to the Port Ludlow ferry.

That made three different stories Monty had told about the night of December 21— one to Lois Hailie, one to the police and yet another to his friend Tony Enos.

———

While awaiting his divorce from Hallie he had spread the word that he and Elinore Pearson were married. There was only one person who knew differently . . . his lawyer, Max Church. And Max Church had succeeded Mr. Smythe as prosecuting attorney in Port Angeles.

Murder was coming home. Perhaps Prosecutor Church knew where it lived when he read the reports. Perhaps he already had the answers when the officers checked on Elinore Pearson. If he did, he took no chances. It took a lot of digging, but Max Church located Mrs. Harry Brooks, owner of a general store near Monty's home.

She told him that just before Christmas, 1937, Monty had borrowed a part of a piece of rope from her.

She still had the other piece of the rope and under microscopic examination it matched the one found tied to Hallie's body!

It was on October 24, 1941, that Monty was arrested, and on February 24 of the following year brought to trial. There were lies then, lies that Monty tried to live up to, a vain attempt to prove that his wife was still alive. Even science almost came to his rescue, but the work the police put into establishing the identity of the murder victim was too air tight, too positive to be smashed. The prosecution fought for the death penalty, but the evidence of the constant fights and Hallie's own prophetic statement that unless she left Monty, one or the other would die, threw doubt on it having been a premeditated murder.

The jury's verdict was guilty of second-degree murder and on March 20, 1942, Monty Illingworth was sentenced to life imprisonment in Washington State Penitentiary.

Nature had foiled a murderer's cunning by allowing

Crescent Lake to give up the missing dead. The irony came at the beginning and was still there at the end . . . Monty had the rare opportunity of hearing the man who had once been his own lawyer present the case against him to a jury that saw fit to put him away for life.

A LOOK AT: STAND UP AND DIE!

BY MICKEY SPILLANE AND MAX ALLAN COLLINS

A BEST-SELLING AUTHOR MICKEY SPILLANE COLLECTION OF LONG-THOUGHT-LOST HARDBOILED TALES.

All of Spillane's classic ingredients—betrayal, sex, gangsters, and, of course, revenge—are in one place for the first time and told in his trademark muscular prose.

Readers familiar with Spillane will revel in the purity of these granite-hard crime stories that provide everything they expect and more from their favorite author. Those new to the works of the biggest selling mystery writer of the 20th century will discover Spillane's one-of-a-kind world of killers, femme fatales, and heroes more dangerous than meat-hook-wielding psychopaths…

A total of ten of Spillane's rarest adventures are included in this collection, so be sure to put it at the top of your must-read list!

Often imitated, never equaled, Mickey Spillane and his creations are always unique and exciting. A true delight for crime fiction fans, this edition is sure to become a collector's item.

Stand Up and Die! includes: Stand Up and Die, Together We Kill, The Girl Behind the Hedge, The Pickpocket, I'll Die Tomorrow, Everybody's Watching Me, Tomorrow I Die, Hot Cat, The Gold Fever Tapes, and Tonight I Die—A Mike Hammer Story.

AVAILABLE MAY 2022

BOOKS BY MICKEY SPILLANE AND MAX ALLAN COLLINS

Dead Street (2007)

ABOUT MICKEY SPILLANE

Mickey Spillane was the best-selling American mystery writer of the 20th century. He introduced Mike Hammer in *I, the Jury* (1947), which sold in the millions, as did the six tough mysteries that soon followed. The controversial P.I. has been the subject of a radio show, comic strip, and several television series, starring Darren McGavin in the 1950s and Stacy Keach in the '80s and '90s. Numerous gritty movies have been made from Spillane novels, notably director Robert Aldrich's seminal film noir, *Kiss Me Deadly* (1955), and *The Girl Hunters* (1963), in which the writer played his own famous hero.

Only a handful of writers in the genre have achieved such superstar status. Spillane's position was unique—reviled by many mainstream critics, despised and envied by a number of his contemporaries in the very field he'd revitalized; but the creator of Mike Hammer had an impact not just on mystery and suspense fiction but popular culture in general.

The success of the reprint editions of his startlingly violent and sexy novels jump-started the paperback original, and his redefinition of the action hero as a tough guy who mercilessly executed villains and who slept with beautiful, willing women remains influential to this day.

The Day the Sea Rolled Back, his first novel for young people, was a Junior Literary Guild Selection. That book, its sequel *The Ship That Never Was*, and a previously unpublished Josh and Larry adventure have been collected by Rough Edges Press as *The Shrinking Island*, offering further proof of Spillane's marvelous ability to hold readers of any age spellbound.

ABOUT MAX ALLAN COLLINS

Max Allan Collins was named a Grand Master in 2017 by the Mystery Writers of America. He is a three-time winner of the Private Eye Writers of America "Shamus" award, receiving the PWA "Eye" for Life Achievement (2006) and their "Hammer" award for making a major contribution to the private eye genre with the Nathan Heller saga (2012).

His graphic novel *Road to Perdition* (1998) became the Academy Award-winning Tom Hanks film, followed by prose sequels and several graphic novels. His other comics credits include the syndicated strip *Dick Tracy*, *Batman*, and his own *Ms. Tree* and *Wild Dog*.

His innovative Quarry novels were adapted as a 2016 TV series by Cinemax. His other suspense series include Eliot Ness, Krista Larson, Reeder and Rogers, and the *Disaster* novels. He has completed twelve Mike Hammer novels begun by the late Mickey Spillane; his audio novel, *Mike Hammer: The Little Death* with Stacy Keach, won a 2011 Audie.

For five years, he was sole licensing writer for TV's *CSI: Crime Scene Investigation* (and its spin-offs), writing best-selling novels, graphic novels, and video games. His tie-in books have appeared on the USA TODAY and *New York Times* bestseller lists, including *Saving Private Ryan*, *Air Force One*, and *American Gangster*.

Collins has written and directed four features and two documentaries, including the Lifetime movie *Mommy*

(1996) and *Mike Hammer's Mickey Spillane* (1998); he scripted *The Expert*, a 1995 HBO World Premiere, and *The Last Lullaby* (2009) from his novel *The Last Quarry*. His Edgar-nominated play *Eliot Ness: An Untouchable Life* (2004) became a PBS special, and he has co-authored two non-fiction books on Ness, *Scarface and the Untouchable* (2018) and *Eliot Ness and the Mad Butcher* (2020).

Collins and his wife, writer Barbara Collins, live in Iowa. As "Barbara Allan," they have collaborated on eighteen novels, including the *Trash 'n' Treasures* mystery, *Antiques Flee Market* (2008), winning the Romantic Times Best Humorous Mystery Novel award of 2009. Their son Nathan has translated numerous novels into English from Japanese, as well as video games and manga.